THE FIGHTER IN UNIT J

Mockingbird Place

LEE SWIFT

Copyright 2016 Lee Swift
Edited by Chloe Vale
Cover Art: Petra Leitner

eBook ISBN: 978-1-937249-17-5

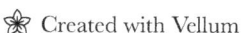 Created with Vellum

This one's for my wonderful niece, Kelsi, who is an aspiring writer. You can do it, sweetheart. Just keep believing in yourself.

Mockingbird Place

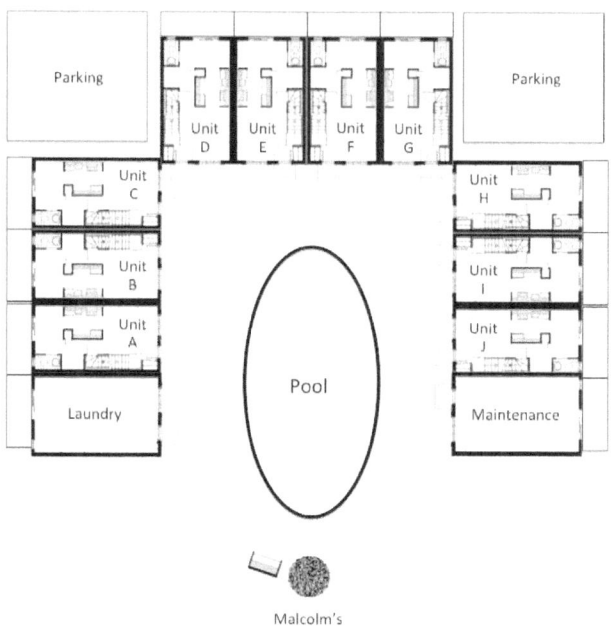

Parking

Unit D · Unit E · Unit F · Unit G

Parking

Unit C

Unit B

Unit A

Laundry

Pool

Unit H

Unit I

Unit J

Maintenance

Malcolm's
Tree

Chapter 1

S tephen Norelli
Friday Night

WHEN ANTHONY TAKES another punch to the gut, I feel my entire body tense up.

His opponent lands one more hit to the side of Anthony's face, and his mouth guard flies out. My heart is pounding hard in my chest.

Damn it, Anthony. When are you going to fight back? This guy is making hamburger meat out of you.

Why am I surprised? This is how all his fights I've seen have gone. He lets his opponent wail on him for several rounds until his body is at the point of utter exhaustion and total pain. And then something strange always happens. He becomes a beast, striking back, and wins the match. Why does he do that? It's obvious he could win most matches in the very first round. But he doesn't. And each time I witness one of his fights I'm even more mystified, like now. I need to find out what's going on inside of him. How else can I help Anthony? How else can there be a chance for us?

The crowd is on its feet cheering. I'm standing but I can't cheer. Hell, I can't even breathe.

Every seat is filled. It's no wonder. Anthony always draws a big crowd when he fights.

Tonight Anthony's opponent is Justin O'Brien, an MMA fighter from New York, who has been climbing up the ranks. O'Brien is slightly taller than Anthony and has red hair and green eyes. His arms are full of tats.

Anthony has two tats that I've seen. A lion on his left upper arm and a tribal symbol on the right.

O'Brian's people have been trying to get a fight with Anthony for several months and were thrilled when he finally became available. Not everyone from Mockingbird Place goes to all of Anthony's matches like me and his brother Nicco, but since this is a championship fight, almost all of our neighbors are here. Nicco has let his hair grow out. He's just an older version of Anthony. Very good looking.

I look at the time. Only ninety seconds left in this fourth five-minute round. This is a title match, so unless one of them is knocked out or disqualified, there will be four more rounds—*four eternities in my mind.*

Until meeting Anthony, I'd never been to an MMA cage fight before. Actually, I'd never been to any kind of fight. Boxing never interested me, nor did wrestling.

Suddenly, Anthony charges the guy, grabs him, and whispers in his ear.

I've been to four of Anthony's matches and seen him do this same thing to each of his opponents. Just like the previous matches after Anthony's whispers, he pummels O'Brien with his fists.

What does he say to them before he knocks them out?

Anthony's fists pound into O'Brien again and again. He's like a monster that has been unleashed. Terrifying. Powerful. Dangerous.

O'Brien stumbles backward, hitting the metal boundary that separates the fans from the fighters, but Anthony is not letting up.

Anthony steps forward and delivers a kick to the side of O'Brien's head.

O'Brien falls to the ground, eyes closed. The referee runs up and declares it a knockout.

It's over.

The crowd roars, chanting, "Tony! Tony! Tony!"

Anthony lifts his gloved hands in victory. He glances at us and winks.

"Anthony's okay." Nicco is sitting next to me.

"Yes, he is." I'm finally able to breathe again.

"Quite the fight, Father Stephen. My little brother is still on top." Nicco just won't call me Stephen no matter how many times I ask him to. Yes, I am an Episcopal priest, but to my friends I prefer just to be called Stephen. Nicco was raised Roman Catholic, so it's difficult for him to call me anything but father.

"Thank God, Anthony isn't hurt," Martha says.

She and Sarah, who we all lovingly call S & M, are sitting behind Nicco and me. Those sweet women are in their seventies but you'd never know it. S & M are vibrant and full of life.

"That's my little brother!" Nicco shouts as Anthony's trainer puts a robe around his shoulders. "Anthony Enzo Mantonvani!"

I love hearing the pride in Nicco's voice. He moved in with Anthony in Unit J when he got out of prison. It feels like that happened ages ago, though it's only been a couple of months now. Nicco went to prison for a murder he didn't commit. Father Grissom and I played a roll in getting his sentence overturned.

I know Anthony is thrilled to have his brother back, but he still feels responsible for the years Nicco lost behind bars. All of us, including Nicco, have tried to convince him that it wasn't his fault. He was only a kid at the time. Nicco's gang killed the man who had been molesting Anthony. None of the gang came forward.

Nicco and I have had many heart-to-heart discussions. He learned that the gang he had been a part of didn't have his back like they claimed. They weren't his brothers. They just let him take the fall.

"Look at Anthony's face, all bloodied and bruised," Sarah says in a concerned tone. She turns to Martha. "Sweetheart, we'll need to get your homemade remedy ready for him when we get home."

Martha smiles and squeezes Sarah's hand. "Already done, S. We'll take care of him as usual."

I don't know what is in Martha's remedy, but it definitely works. Anthony heals so fast. Except for a couple of scars, which only add to his sexiness, his face is flawless. From the very first moment I saw Anthony he took my breath away. I'd never seen anyone as handsome as him in my whole life. Dark, thick wavy hair that I would love to run my fingers through. Sexy mouth that is so kissable. Big brown eyes with long lashes that I could easily lose myself in.

When I told Anthony that my church affirms same-sex marriages, even with priests and bishops, he was taken aback. Is that why he has pulled away from me? Does he already know I have feelings for him? I've tried to keep my heart in check whenever I'm around him. He has too much to deal with right now. If there is any chance of us starting a relationship, it will have to come later. But I'm not giving up hope that the timing will be right one day and we'll be together.

Anthony's and my eyes lock for a moment.

Once again I witness the awe and calm from him that only comes after he's beaten an opponent like O'Brien.

The crowd noise quiets as the medical team surrounds O'Brien, who is still not moving. Anthony turns around and faces his fallen opponent. His eyes widen in shock, and the look of awe and calm I'd seen just a moment ago vanishes.

"He's okay, isn't he?" Anthony asks the EMT, dread filling every syllable.

"Step back, sir," the man tells him.

The announcer's voice comes over the speakers. "Everyone, please remain seated. The medical staff will be transporting Mr. O'Brien to the hospital."

Two more men rush in with a stretcher.

Not a good sign.

Nicco turns to me. "Father Stephen, Anthony needs us."

"Yes, he does. Let's go."

As Nicco and I step up to the cage, I think about all the times I've tried to reach Anthony. He has so many demons from the past that he struggles with that I haven't been able to break through his walls. But I refuse to give up.

"Anthony," Nicco calls to him, "it's going to be okay."

Anthony doesn't turn around. He seems to be in a daze as the EMTs hoist O'Brien onto the stretcher. Finally, Anthony does look at us.

My heart rips apart seeing the pain on his face. He's been through so much his entire life.

Please, God. Don't let O'Brien die. That would ruin Anthony for sure.

That isn't how a priest should pray. I am concerned for O'Brien, but my heart is for Anthony. It has been for quite some time. *Only you, God, know how much I love him.*

Anthony comes out of the cage. "I need a ride to the hospital now. I have to be sure O'Brien is okay."

The panic in his voice is difficult to hear.

"Don't worry about it," I tell him. "I'll take you."

"I have to get S & M back home," Nicco says as the ladies walk up next to us. "They rode with me here. But I'll meet you at the hospital after."

"You're not taking us home, Niccolo," Martha states firmly. "We're going to the hospital with you."

"Okay, then." Anthony rushes to follow the stretcher out the back of the building.

Racing to the parking lot, I shout after him. "I'll grab my car to pick you up by the ambulance."

As I run to my Jeep Cherokee, my mind is racing. I have to help Anthony get through this any way I can. Even though he's been distant with me, taking him to the hospital is one way I can help him.

I drive around back just as the EMTs are loading O'Brien into the ambulance. Still wearing his robe, Anthony looks even more distraught than ever. He jumps inside my car as the ambulance drives out of the parking lot. I'm shocked to see big tears in his eyes, something I've never seen before from him. Anthony always presents this tough-guy act to everyone. I realized shortly after I met him that it was only a façade. Anthony has a huge heart, even though he tries to hide it from the world, from his neighbors and friends, from Nicco, *and from me*. But I've witnessed how kind he can be, especially to S & M.

"I asked them if I could ride in the ambulance but they said I couldn't. I would be in the way. They don't get it. I was the one who hurt him. God, I hope he doesn't die."

"O'Brien is in good hands, Anthony. He's going to be okay." *Please God. Let him be okay.*

Chapter 2

Once I park my Jeep at the hospital, Anthony and I race to the emergency room. Nicco and S & M are right behind us. The ambulance arrived just a moment before we did. Anthony follows the EMTs and stretcher through the first set of double doors inside the ER.

It's obvious to me how anxious Anthony is feeling about O'Brien's condition.

When they come to the second set of double doors with a sign that reads "Authorized Personnel," one of the EMTs says to him, "This is as far as you can go, sir."

O'Brien's trainer is standing next to the double doors. I guess him to be in his early sixties, with thinning gray hair and a gray mustache.

He turns and glares at Anthony. "What the hell are you doing here?"

"Why wouldn't I be here?" It's obvious from Anthony's tone that his walls are back up. "I'm the one who hit him."

"That's the very reason you shouldn't be here, Mantonvani. O'Brien's fiancée is just minutes away. The last person she needs to see is the man who put her future husband in the hospital."

"Look, Joe, O'Brien knew what he was getting himself into. We're fighters. We take the risk. I just want to make sure he can fight again."

It's plain to me that Anthony is in his tough-guy mode. Gone are the tears of compassion that were welling up in his eyes earlier.

"Listen to me, Mantonvani. I've been a trainer for years and this is the first time I've ever seen anything like this—a fighter showing up at the hospital of his opponent. It's crazy."

Not wanting Anthony to sink deeper into himself, I decide it's time for me to step in. I extend my hand to the trainer. "Sir, I'm Father Stephen Norelli from the Episcopal Church of the Beloved Disciple."

He shakes my hand. "I'm Joe Merrell…Father." Joe seems skeptical of me. No wonder. I'm not wearing my collar. "Are you here with him?" He points at Anthony.

"I am, and I can assure you that we are only here to make sure that Mr. O'Brien is going to be okay. I would like to have the chance to go in and pray with him, if it's okay with you and his fiancée. In the meantime, Anthony and I will sit over here, out of the way."

Joe's eyes soften. He glances at Anthony. "Is that true? You're only here to make sure O'Brien is going to be okay?"

"Why else would I be here?" Anthony's tone is sarcastic, which is something I've heard many times. It's a defensive tactic he often uses. He lets out a long sigh and his tone softens. "I don't even know O'Brien, but he put up quite the fight. He and I have one thing in common—he's a fighter, just like me. I respect that."

I'm surprised to see Joe nod. He seems satisfied with Anthony words, despite the tone. Is Joe seeing right through Anthony, like me? He just said he's been in the business for years, so he must've been around a lot of fighters with chips on their shoulders and something to prove. *Just like my Anthony.*

My Anthony? I can only hope that might be true one day.

Joe turns to me. "Father, it's your job to make sure this guy doesn't get out of hand. Okay?"

"You've got a deal." I look at Anthony. "Let's go sit down with Nicco and S & M."

"Sure, boss." Anthony marches past me to the waiting area.

"You have your hands full with that one, Father," Joe says.

"Yes, I do, but he's worth it."

"Please say a prayer for O'Brien." Joe's voice cracks with emotion. "He's a good kid, just like your Mantonvani." It seems that Joe did see through Anthony's walls.

"I've already been praying for him, Joe." I place my hand on the man's shoulder. "Hang in there. O'Brien is in good hands now."

I walk into the waiting area, and per Anthony's normal, he's chosen a seat away from everyone else. He's in one of those moods where it's best to just let him be. *For now.*

Sarah waves me over. Nicco is sitting between her and Martha.

I take the seat next to Sarah.

She whispers to me, "I'm so worried about Anthony. He's always been a little moody, but I've never seen him like this before. Do you think you can help him, fath...um...Stephen? I still have trouble calling you by your name and not father. I just wasn't raised that way."

I can't help but grin. She's one of the sweetest women I know. "Sarah, this is the twenty-first century. It's perfectly fine to call me Stephen, especially since I gave you permission to do so, but if it makes you feel better calling me father, then be my guest."

She nods.

I take another quick glance at Anthony and then turn back to her, Martha, and Nicco. "I will try my best to help him, but he's been very distant with me for some time. I was actually surprised when he agreed to let me take him to the hospital."

Martha looks at me with her sage eyes. "Sweetheart, that's his way. The closer someone gets to Anthony the harder it is for him. Opening up isn't something he's ever done except for S and I, and that hasn't been very much."

Nicco sighs. "You can't blame him. Especially after all he's been through."

I'm still overwhelmed with how strong the brotherly bond is between Anthony and Nicco. I never had any brothers or sisters, though when I was a kid I fantasized often what it might be like.

I see a young woman walk into the ER and go straight to O'Brien's trainer. He gives her a comforting hug.

"Who is she?" Nicco asks.

"I believe that's O'Brien's fiancée." Seeing her tears, I'm certain she must be.

"Poor thing," S & M say in unison.

Martha sighs. "She must be worried sick."

Anthony looks up at her. The darkness that spreads over his face tells me that he realizes who she is too.

"I know it may be useless, but I can't let Anthony sit there all alone." I stand. "Excuse me."

Sarah winks at me. "Go, Stephen. We'll be right here if you need us."

I walk over to Anthony, wondering how he will respond to me. It's been difficult these past several months. We had gotten so close before, but then he completely shut me out. When I leaned over to kiss him that pivotal night—that was the cause of all this trouble. I thought we were moving in that direction. Turns out, I was completely wrong.

I don't want to poke the bear, as they say, but I also don't want to just let him suffer.

He looks up at me with those big beautiful brown eyes and I feel my entire body go numb. "Hey. Mind if I sit next to you?"

"Sure." His single syllable is filled with so much meaning for me. He's not pushing me away.

He could have said something sarcastic like "It's a free country" or "I don't own the chairs here." Or he could have just shaken his head no. Or he could have got up and walked away without saying a word. Or a million other responses that would have told me he wasn't interested in my company or anything I had to say.

But he didn't.

I'm probably putting to much meaning into his response of "sure," but I can't help it because it's what I want.

I sit down next to him, thinking about squeezing his hand to reassure him. Of course I don't.

Baby steps, Father Stephen. No touch. Just words of comfort.

"Anthony, everything is going to be fine. O'Brien is going to be okay."

He stands and glares at me. "How the hell do you know he's going to be okay...*Father*? Has God talked to you about this or are you just winging it as usual?"

Damn, I blew it already. I take a deep breath. "Calm down. I understand how you feel."

Remaining standing, his unblinking eyes narrow, zeroing in on me like a hot laser. "How can you understand how I feel? Have you ever been in my shoes? Did you have a mother who loved her drugs more than her sons? Were you raped night after night by her boyfriend? You...with the white collar, everything going right in your world? You don't understand a damn thing, and you definitely don't understand me."

Shocked at how strong he lashed out at me, I watch him storm out of the waiting room. Nicco follows.

Tears well up in my eyes. How am I ever going to be able to help Anthony now?

No. I've never been in his shoes, but I do know a thing or two about how lost and alone a child can feel.

S & M come over to me.

"I'm so sorry, sweetheart," Martha says.

Sarah sits down in the chair Anthony just vacated. "He'll calm down. He always does."

"But this is different." I close my eyes and say a quick prayer. "What happens if O'Brien doesn't—"

"Father," Joe says, causing me to open my eyes.

"Yes. How's your fighter?"

He smiles. "He's going to be okay. It's only a concussion and two broken ribs. The doctor wants to keep him a few days for observation, but he'll be on his feet in no time at all."

"Oh, thank God." Martha hugs me. "Our prayers were answered."

Joe nods and looks at me. "I told O'Brien about you. He and his fiancée would like you to come and pray with them, if you don't mind."

"Of course I don't mind." I turn to S & M. "Please let Anthony know about O'Brien."

"We'll tell him," Sarah says.

"I'll be right back." I stand, and Joe leads me to O'Brien's room. Every step down the hallway all I can think about is Anthony. I hope once he learns that O'Brien is going to be okay that he'll also be okay with me.

When Joe and I walk into the hospital room, I'm stunned at all the bandages on O'Brien. Anthony really did a number on this guy. Still, O'Brien is sitting up in the bed. His fiancée is next to him, smiling ear to ear and holding his hand.

"This is Father Stephen," Joe says. "Father, this is Justin and his fiancée, Melinda."

"Thank you for your prayers, Father," O'Brien says in a thick New York accent. "It obviously worked. I'm feeling great. Would you mind praying one more time? I want to make sure I get out of here tomorrow."

"Justin, you're not getting out of here until the doctors say you can. Period," Melinda states firmly in a Texas accent.

"But Mel, I'm so anxious to get married."

"I'm not marrying you until your face heals up." She grins. "We have the wedding pictures to think about. What would our children think when they look at the photos of our special day and you have two black eyes?" Melinda turns to me. "Father, I agree with Justin. We need your prayers. Would you pray for patience for me and for him to listen to the doctors?"

I smile. "Of course."

After I say the prayer, it's very clear how much O'Brien and Melinda care about each other. I want that for Anthony and me someday. *Wishful thinking?* Probably. I always seem to say or do the wrong thing that sets him off.

I think about the fight that sent O'Brien to the hospital. "Justin, do you mind if I ask you a question?"

"I don't mind at all. What do you want to know?"

"Do you remember what Anthony…I mean Mantonvani whispered to you during the fight?"

"You mean before he beat me to a pulp? How could I forget?" O'Brien takes in a deep breath. "It was crazy. I thought I had him. Three rounds, I had the upper hand. But now I know he was just… hell, I don't know what he was doing. He's an incredible fighter. It was weird what he said to me."

"O'Brien, please get to the point," Joe says. "What were Mantonvani's exact words to you?"

"He said, 'You'll never hurt me again, you fucking pedophile.' Sorry, Father, but his words, not mine. What the hell did he mean by that? I'm no pedophile. I swear."

"I know that, Justin." My gut tightens, realizing what Anthony does when he faces an opponent.

He must be battling the monster that violated his innocence in his mind. But why doesn't he fight back in the early rounds? It doesn't make sense, but I intend to find out.

Anxious to see how Anthony is now that he likely knows O'Brien is okay, I say, "It's been very nice talking with you, but I must be going now. Justin, I'm very glad you're okay."

"Father, we would love for you to come to our wedding, if you can," Melinda says. "Mom and Dad live in Grapevine. That's where Justin and I plan on having the ceremony. I'll let you know when we have the exact date set up."

I tell them I would love too and then I say my good-byes.

When I get back to the waiting room, I find Nicco and S & M, but no Anthony.

"Where is he?" I ask them.

"We don't know," Nicco says. "I tried to catch up with him but he wasn't in the mood to talk. And when my little brother doesn't want to talk, he knows how to disappear. I lost him at the elevators."

I bring out my phone.

Martha touches my arm. "He's not answering, Stephen. We've all tried to call."

Chapter 3

S tanding in the waiting room with Nicco, Sarah, and Martha, I realize that we have to let Anthony know that O'Brien is okay. "Did you try to text him?"

They all shake their heads.

I quickly type a message to him on my phone.

O'Brien is going to be fine.

I stare at my phone, praying he'll respond. My phone buzzes. "Anthony just texted me back."

I can see the relief wash over their faces. I feel it too.

I read Anthony's text. *O'Brien is really ok?*

Yes. Where are you? I ask.

I watch as dots cross the screen, indicating he is responding. *Ubered back to the arena.*

Want me to come get you?

My phone doesn't buzz for several seconds, which drives me crazy. Have I blown it again with him?

Sure.

There's that word again, the one that I put way too much meaning in to. But I can't help myself. At least he's open enough to let me give him a ride.

"So, what did he text to you?" Nicco asks.

I hold out my phone for him and S & M to see. "I'll go get him now."

"As soon as you can, bring him to our place," Martha says. "I want to get some salve on his cuts and bruises ASAP."

"Of course."

"But don't hurry. M's salve can wait a little longer." Sarah leans forward. It's clear she has a point to make. "If he wants time alone with you, Stephen, take all you need."

"I agree with that," Nicco says. "You're good for my brother, even though he may not realize it yet."

What does he mean by that? Good as a priest? A friend? Or is it possible that Nicco thinks I would be a good boyfriend for Anthony? Whatever he means, I want to be there for him.

The four of us walk out of the hospital together. Nicco leads S & M to his car. I rush to mine.

When I arrive back at the arena, Anthony is standing outside. He's changed into his street clothes and is holding his gym bag. God, he looks so sexy. Even though I know this is serious, I am thrilled to have a chance to spend time with him alone. It really sounds stupid, selfish, and even silly to me, but it is honestly how I feel. Every second I get to be with him is a moment I treasure.

He hops inside my car. "Is O'Brien awake? How long do the doctors think he has to stay in the hospital? Will he be able to fight again?" These are the most words I've heard him string together in a single breath.

"Whoa, Anthony. One question at a time, please. Yes, O'Brien is awake. I don't think he'll have to stay in the hospital more than a day or two. O'Brien says he will fight again, although I don't know what his doctors say about that."

"Oh. You've talked to him?" Anthony's eyes are bright with excitement.

"I have. He's a nice guy and so are his fiancée, Melinda, and his trainer, Joe."

"You need to get me to the hospital. I want to see him for myself."

"Anthony, it's two in the morning. O'Brien is probably sleeping."

"I don't care if he's asleep. I'll wait until he's awake. But I want to go. Are you going to take me or do I need to Uber back?" His impatient tone is cutting.

"Of course, I'll take you." I pull away from the arena, wondering if I'll ever be able to break through Anthony's walls.

Fifteen minutes later, I pull into the very same spot that I was parked in earlier. Anthony opens the door and rushes to the entrance without waiting for me. I get out and race to catch up with him. The last thing I want to happen is a scene between him and O'Brien. I know what Anthony wants from this meeting, but I also know that it could get out of hand. I'm going to do my best to keep that from happening.

I catch up with Anthony at the elevators. "What's your hurry?"

"I don't know, Stephen." He sighs. "Hell, I don't even know what room they put O'Brien in."

"Room 427."

The elevator doors open, and Anthony and I enter together.

I can tell he's nervous from the way he's fidgeting.

The doors open, and once again without waiting for me, Anthony exits the elevator, heading the wrong direction.

"Anthony, it's this way."

He turns around. "Oh. Okay."

I lead him straight to the room. Anthony did promise to wait to talk to O'Brien if he was asleep. God, I hope that's how we find him, because that will give Anthony time to calm his nerves. But that isn't the case. When we round the corner, I see the door is open and the light is on.

Before we get to room 427, Joe walks out. His eyes widen when he sees Anthony.

"What the hell are you doing here again? Go home, Tony. This isn't—"

"It's okay, Joe." O'Brien's voice is strong and steady. "Let him come in. I want to talk to Tony."

Though I can't see O'Brien from where I'm standing, I can see Melinda is in the chair inside the room.

She yawns, clearly having just been asleep. "Sweetheart, do you need something?"

"I'm fine, honey, but we do have company."

Joe leans forward to Anthony, eyes narrowing. In a low tone he says, "You fuck with him and you will regret it, understand?"

"Just here to make sure he's okay, Joe," Anthony says. "That's all."

He doesn't wait for him to say anything else, but walks past him into the room. Joe and I are right behind him.

O'Brien looks even stronger than when I prayed with him earlier. Melinda jumps up to the side of his bed. She stands in a protective way next to him. Anthony seems oblivious to everyone except O'Brien.

"Are you going to be able to fight again, O'Brien?" Anthony blurts out. "I have to know."

"You should already know that, Mantonvani. I'm a fighter, just like you. Of course I'll be in the cage again. Fighting is in my DNA."

Anthony nods. "That's all I need to know."

He turns to walk away.

"Wait." O'Brien calls after Anthony. "I need to ask *you* a question. Do you really think I'm a pedophile?"

Anthony turns around and looks him square in the eye. "No. I don't." His words are clipped and sharp. Once again he moves to leave the room.

"Then why did you say that to me when we were fighting?"

"It's a long story that I don't intend to go into."

O'Brien's tone deepens, matching Anthony's. "You owe it to me, Mantonvani. I deserve to know."

"Maybe some day I'll tell you over a couple of beers." Anthony glances at me for a millisecond and then turns his attention back to O'Brien. "But not now."

He walks out.

This meeting could have been so much worse, but Anthony kept his cool by staying in control.

"What's wrong with him?" Melinda asks.

"Nothing, sweetheart," O'Brien answers, grabbing her hand. "Tony is a fighter, just like me. It's our way."

"Get some sleep," I tell them and hurry once again to catch Anthony.

The elevator doors close before I can enter. He's gone. I punch the down button over and over, anxious to get to him. I don't know if he'll wait for me. Why should he? What help have I been to him? Just a taxi driver. Anything I say or do seems to make things worse instead of better.

When I exit the hospital I expect to see him riding off in an Uber car. But I don't. Instead, he's standing next to my car, waiting for me.

Okay, Stephen. Don't say anything stupid. Just listen.

When I step up to him, I see a big grin on his face.

"You were right, Stephen. O'Brien is going to be okay. He's really going to be okay." He wraps his arms around me and to my utter shock, presses his lips to mine.

Chapter 4

I feel my knees weaken as Anthony deepens the kiss. This is what I've been dreaming of—him letting me know that he's interested in more than just friendship with me.

Is this really happening?

Suddenly, he pulls away from me and takes a couple of steps back. "I'm…I'm…sorry. I…shouldn't have done that, Father Stephen."

"Damn it, Anthony. Can't you see past my collar, which by the way I'm not wearing right now?" I can feel the heat and desire that his thick lips awakened inside me. Now that he's shutting down once again, I'm even more frustrated than ever. "I'm a man, Anthony. Not a saint. Yes, I'm a priest, but that doesn't change how I feel about you. I like you. I like you very much. I would like to get closer to you. Much closer."

"But you are a priest. That changes things."

"Why? My church doesn't care. In fact it celebrates love to everyone, regardless if it's a man and woman, a woman and woman, or like us, a man and man." I sigh, seeing him take another step back. My words are falling on his deaf ears. I'm just pushing him further away. "But you and I have talked about this before.

Maybe you aren't able to see me as a man. Maybe you can only see me as a priest. Or is it something else that is keeping us apart?"

He looks me directly in the eyes, and his words come out in the same old matter-of-fact tone. "I don't need to be in a relationship with anyone. Can we go now or should I get Uber?"

"I'll take you back to Mockingbird Place." I have no doubt that he can read the look on my face and see how sad he's made me.

We get in the car without another word. The entire way home neither of us utter a single word. The silence crushes me, and I feel my heart ripping apart. Why did he kiss me? Was it just the exuberance of knowing O'Brien was okay? Or was it something else? Something deeper? Here I go with the wishful thinking again. Whatever it is I'm clearly not the person who will get him to face his demons.

I pull into the parking lot of Mockingbird Place, our 10-unit Mediterranean complex. "I know it's late but S & M made me promise to have you come by their apartment so they can apply Martha's salve to your cuts."

"I'll go, Stephen. Goodnight." He gets out of my car and walks away.

I pull out the key but remain inside my car.

There will be no sleeping for me tonight. I'm too wound up. All I can think about is Anthony's incredible kiss. I wish there was someone I could talk to. Father Grissom comes to mind. He's in town visiting his niece, but it's three in the morning. I'm sure he's sound asleep.

I put the key back in the ignition. When I'm this stressed one of the best remedies is enjoying a big slice of pie. I drive to my favorite diner, Aunt Lucy's, which is just a few blocks away. The pie doesn't fix anything, but it sure does make me forget for a little while.

When I walk into the retro-style diner, I hear someone call my name.

"Father Stephen, over here." Maddox motions to me. He and Jaris are sitting together at a table. They both have coffee and are holding menus. "Join us."

They're both doctors and live in Unit H at Mockingbird Place.

Their relationship is proof that love sometimes can overcome the most difficult obstacles. Maybe it isn't impossible for Anthony and me. Or maybe I'm being delusional again.

Not wanting to be alone right now, I walk over to their table, grateful to see some friendly faces.

I take a seat. "Why are you two guys up so late?"

"Jaris and I were called into the hospital because of a pileup on 635. What happened to Anthony's opponent? What was his name?"

Jaris answers, "O'Brien, right?"

"Right. O'Brien is doing fine. He has a slight concussion and a couple of broken ribs. He'll be back on his feet in a few weeks."

"Good to hear," Jaris says. "What about you? Why are you out this late? Did you get called out for an emergency too, Father?"

"Guys, you know you can call me Stephen."

They say in unison. "Okay, Stephen."

I smile. "No emergency. Just couldn't sleep."

"I don't mean to pry, Stephen, but from the look on your face it seems like there's a reason you couldn't sleep." Jaris takes a sip of his coffee.

Seeing the waitress headed our direction, I say, "You're very intuitive, Doc."

"Hi, fellas," the waitress says. "I see someone new has joined you. Would you like coffee too?" She hands me a menu.

"I would, but I don't need a menu," I answer. "I'm just dying to have a thick slice of chocolate cream pie."

"Mm. I hadn't thought about having pie," Maddox says, handing his menu back to her. "Make it two."

"Actually, three," Jaris adds.

"You got it."

As she walks away, Jaris leans forward. "Well, Stephen, how can we help you? We're all from Mockingbird Place, and you know what that means."

Maddox smiles. "Of course he does, sweetheart. We all get into each other's business, but we only do it out of concern for one another."

"We're more than just a community," I say. "We're family."

Feeling more relaxed I tell them everything that happened with Anthony. "I don't know why he pulled away after he kissed me. I'm very confused."

"I don't want to give you false hope," Maddox says, "but it's obvious to me that Tony has feelings for you."

"Strong feelings," Jaris adds. "In fact, we thought you were already a couple, just keeping it quiet for now."

"I wish that were the case, but it isn't. I don't know if Anthony will ever want to be with me."

Jaris pushes his cup to the side. "So, are you giving up?"

His question cuts me to the core, especially knowing all he and Maddox had to overcome to be together. "No. I'm not giving up. I simply don't know what to do."

"I didn't know what to do either, but I believe that if you love someone and you are patient, everything will eventually work out." Jaris takes Maddox's hand. "It did for us."

Maddox says, "Just believe, Stephen. Believe in you and Anthony."

"Thanks, guys. It's no accident that we ran into each other. This is exactly what I needed to hear. I won't give up on Anthony or me or us. We belong together. That's a fact. Anthony just needs to figure it out for himself."

The waitress brings my coffee and our three pies.

We continue talking about all sorts of subjects, from politics to religion, from the state of the economy to our favorite band, Red Shimmer, to all sorts of things. But mostly we talk about how happy we are living at Mockingbird Place.

WHEN I PULL into my parking space at the complex, the sky is getting lighter as the sun begins to rise. I should be exhausted after staying up all night but I'm not. Instead I feel energized.

After talking with Jaris and Maddox, I'm even more determined not to give up on Anthony and me. The two of us need to talk. I have some things I must say to him. But it's only six in the morning.

I'm sure he's asleep. And I still have to put together a sermon for tomorrow's service.

As I head to my back patio gate, I bump into Harvey, the complex's maintenance man. He's quite wealthy and only does this job because he loves the people here so much.

"Hi, Stephen," he says with his usual big smile. I think he's close to eighty years old, but you definitely could never tell it. In fact, he and his boyfriend just met a few months ago and are like two lovesick teenagers.

"Hey, Harvey. Starting early today I see."

"Yes, I am. It's the big day. I have a lot to get done."

I clearly have overlooked something important. "Big day?"

"Don't tell me you've already forgotten about the party at my house."

"Oh, yeah. It is Saturday. Your party to honor Malcolm is tonight. Today is his birthday."

Malcolm passed away some time ago but is beloved by most of the residents. He was Harvey's best friend and owned Mockingbird Place until he died.

"You're coming, aren't you?" he asks.

"Yes, I am. What would you like me to bring?"

"Not a thing. My guy and I have everything covered. It's going to be a blast just like Malcolm would have wanted. I heard about Tony's fight from S & M. Glad his opponent is doing better. I wish we could have been there, but with this party and our trip to Spain next week, we just couldn't make it."

"Trip to Spain?"

He grins. "Yep. It's our six-month anniversary. So we're flying off for a romantic week in Barcelona."

"Harvey, don't you think it's time you and Nathan got married?"

"Oh, we're too old for that."

"You're never too old for love. You know that."

He pats me on the shoulder. "You're giving this old man something to think about…young man. What about you? I see how you look at Tony whenever you're in the same room."

"I bet you've never seen him looking at me the same way."

"Oh, yes I have. I may be old but I'm not blind."

I'm shocked to hear that. "You have? Really?"

Harvey chuckles. "Many times. And not just me. The whole complex has noticed you two. You and Anthony are all we talk about these days. I wouldn't be surprised if we didn't start taking bets when you two are finally going to get together." He winks. "If you know what I mean…Father."

I smile. "Yes, I know what you mean, but Anthony and I aren't on the same page right now. I want to talk to him but I'm not sure how to approach the subject of us dating."

"You get right to the point. It's really easy. When you get my age, you don't beat around the bush. You just go for it."

"I don't think that would go well. I'm afraid if I told him how I feel, it will blow up in my face. Anthony might shut me out. Now, we're at least talking." I open my gate. "Do you have time for a quick cup of coffee? I sure could use some of your sage advice."

"I would love a cup, and I've got some donuts in my pickup. I have to hide them from you-know-who. I love him but he's such a health nut I have to sneak my treats."

I laugh. "Why not? If I look as good as you do at your age after eating a few donuts along the way, I'll be very happy."

"Sounds like we're starting the party early." He looks up into the sky. "Malcolm, you old devil. I wish you were here. But it's okay. I'm going to eat your portion for you." He looks back at me. "I'll be right in."

He walks to his truck.

I open my back door and put on a pot of coffee.

Harvey comes into my kitchen with a dozen donuts. "Let's get this party going. There's four chocolates, four Boston creams, and four maples."

"Sounds delicious." I fill two mugs with steaming hot coffee. "You take cream or sugar?"

"Just black. Thanks."

We sit down at my table.

"Stephen, have you heard about the two bald guys who put their heads together and made an ass out of themselves?" Harvey always makes us laugh with his silly jokes. He tells the same ones over and over again, but they are still just as funny as the first time we heard them.

After two donuts and two cups of coffee each, and several more jokes, we lean back in our chairs.

"So, Stephen, have you had enough to drink to tell me what's going on between you and Tony, or should we break out the sacramental wine?"

I laugh, feeling completely at ease with him. "Have you ever thought about being a priest, Harvey? You definitely could hold everyone's attention."

"Priest? No. Bishop or pope? Sure. Seriously, talk to me. What are you worried about with Tony?"

I tell him about what happened at the fight. And the kiss. "I keep getting mixed signals from him, and I'm not sure…well…I don't know…it's just that…"

He grins. "Spit it out, son, before you choke on it."

I laugh. "I'm able to be very clear with everything in my life except when it comes to Anthony. I just can't seem to form a complete sentence."

"Remind me sometime to tell you the joke about the three tongue-tied priests, but for now, listen up. It's not what you say but what you do. You just have to love him, and keep loving him. No matter what. And when Tony needs a soft, safe place to fall, he'll come to you. Trust me."

"Thanks, Harvey. I do love him with all my heart. I couldn't stop loving him even if I tried."

My doorbell rings, and I look at the time on my phone. 6:55 a.m.

"Who could that be at this hour?"

Chapter 5

I leave my chair. "Excuse me. I'll be right back."

Harvey stands. "That's okay, Stephen. I need to get busy. My guy is expecting me home to help set up the party."

I pick up the box with the rest of the donuts. "Don't forget to take these."

"That's okay. You keep them." He smiles. "I don't want to get caught."

As the doorbell rings again, I place the box back on the table.

"Besides, your company may want some. Don't forget what I told you." He winks at me and walks out my back door.

When I open my front door, I find Anthony standing on my steps and instantly feel my heart racing. I was hoping for more time to figure out what I should say to him, but it looks like the ball is in Anthony's court now. Regardless what he's come to say I won't forget what Harvey just told me. Or what Maddox and Jaris said to me at the diner. *I won't give up on us.*

"I know it's early, but may I come in?" Anthony asks.

"Sure. Want some coffee? I also have donuts."

"I would love donuts and coffee. That would be great."

We walk to my table. I pick up Harvey's and my mugs. "Have a seat."

Anthony's eyes narrow slightly. "I hope I haven't interrupted something."

"Not at all. It was just Harvey."

His eyes widen and his lips curl up into a slight smile. "Oh. It was just Harvey."

Did Anthony think I had an overnight guest? Was he jealous?

I hope so.

He sits down at the table and looks inside the donut box. "Yum. Chocolate icing with sprinkles is my favorite kind of donut."

I grin, adding that to my list of things that are special about him. "Harvey wanted to remind me about Malcolm's party tonight. Are you going?"

"Yes, I plan on going. Malcolm meant the world to me. I have no idea what would have happened if Malcolm hadn't stepped in to help me after Nicco went to prison." He pulls out two donuts. "Mind if I have a couple?"

"Knock yourself out." I get a fresh mug and fill it and mine with coffee. "You know I've never met Malcolm but I've heard so many good things about him. Do you mind telling me what he did for you?" I sit down next to him.

"He was the sweetest man I've ever known. When Nicco and Maddox were in prison, Nicco told Maddox about my situation, which was pretty awful. My mom was worthless, totally lost to her drug addiction."

No wonder he is having trouble forgiving his mother after all the horror he had to endure because of her.

"I left and ended up on the streets, another lost teenager in Dallas. Maddox reached out to Malcolm, whom he'd known since he was a kid. Malcolm didn't hesitate to help. When he found me I was starving and dirty. He bought me the best hamburger I've ever had in my life, and some fries and a chocolate milk shake. I'll never forget it. When he was sure I was full, he invited me back to his home at Mockingbird Place. I met Oliver, who he also had rescued from the streets. I got a nice hot shower and they washed my clothes."

"But didn't you end up living with S & M?"

He nods. "They came over that very first night. I instantly clicked with them. I don't know why, but I did. Maybe it was because I'd never had a real mother, someone who cared about me unconditionally. And, God knows, S & M have the biggest hearts in the world. They invited me to their place for the night, and I never left until I turned eighteen and got the unit next to theirs."

"Nicco told me that Malcolm was the one who introduced you to MMA fighting."

"That's right. I had so much anger inside me." He grins. "More than now, if you can believe that. Malcolm and S & M knew I needed an outlet. So, Malcolm took me to a gym that a friend of his owned. He gave me a pair of boxing gloves and placed me in front of a heavy bag. I stood there like a…well, Martha would say like a knot on a log. Malcolm kept telling me to hit the bag, but I just would barely tap it. He continued encouraging me to hit it harder and harder, saying 'Reach down deep, Tony, and pull out all the anger inside of you. Let it out of your fists and onto that bag.'"

I can see that Anthony is reliving that moment right in front of me, so I don't dare say a word lest I break the spell.

He stares into his empty cup. "I started hitting it harder and harder and harder. The heavy bag was no longer just a bag but transformed into my mother's boyfriend, who raped me when I was just a kid. The tears burned in my eyes and I started yelling 'I'm going to kill you, asshole. You're dead. Dead. Dead.' Malcolm pulled me into his arms and held me tight. I was so lost that I just kept pounding away on him. He didn't let go and said, 'Let it all out, son. Let it go.' I don't know how long I kept hitting Malcolm and crying. But however long it was he just kept holding onto me." He looks up from his cup to me. "Malcolm was the only man I ever trusted."

"Anthony, that's a wonderful story. I would like to honor Malcolm tomorrow, since he was a member of my church for so many years. All the congregation talks about what a great man he was. I'm sorry I never met him. Would you mind if I mentioned him in my sermon?"

"Malcolm would be pleased and so would I."

I see pain in Anthony's eyes for the things he's had to suffer for so long. I want to do something, say something. *But what?*

"I still have anger issues, Stephen. I probably always will. That's why I became an MMA fighter. It's the one thing that lets me stay sane. But look what happened last night. I could've killed O'Brien."

"But you didn't. He's going to be fine."

"But what about the next time? I'm not sure I should ever go back in that cage. But if I don't, I know the anger will build up inside me and I'll go crazy. I don't know what to do."

"Let me help you figure it out."

He shakes his head. "I'm not normal. Far from it. I couldn't sleep thinking about our kiss last night. You're a wonderful man but I can't let my baggage ruin your life."

I lean forward, feeling frustrated that we're headed down the same old road. "Don't, Anthony."

"Don't what?"

"Don't shut me out. I'm not going anywhere. I'm here for you."

Anthony pushes the box and mug to the side. "You can't waste a single day on a loser like me. You deserve so much more."

I reach across the table for his hand, but he pulls back. "Anthony, you're not a loser. Not even close. You were a kid and survived hell. You're strong. You're kind. You're loyal. You're amazing. And I know I'm already falling in love with you."

He slams his fists on the table. "No! You can't!"

I slam my fists on the table. "Oh. Yes. I. Can. And I do."

Anthony jumps up so fast that the chair turns over. "No. No. This is not happening…*Father* Stephen."

He marches out the door.

I want to go after him, but I know at this point it won't do any good. I need to let him calm down—*once again*. Is this how it's going to be between us from now on? On again and off again. Hot and cold. Over and over. I don't know, but what I do know is I care deeply for him. I just want it to work out for us.

No matter what, I'm not giving up.

Chapter 6

I can't stop thinking about how Anthony and I left things. I've tried to text him, but he isn't texting me back.

It's no wonder it was so hard to finish my sermon with Anthony on my mind. Even after hearing his story about Malcolm it still took me four hours to type the last sentence of my sermon. That's a new record.

I hit the print button on my laptop. I hope my words will honor Malcolm's memory. He was such a great man and helped so many. Like Anthony.

I went over and knocked on Anthony's door when I needed a break. Nicco answered and told me that he'd left hours earlier to go back to the hospital to check on O'Brien. He's probably still very concerned about him. Until O'Brien is released, I'm certain he will continue to be.

I asked Nicco to have Anthony call me when he got back. But my phone hasn't rung even once.

There's nothing else for me to do but wait this out. I hope Anthony comes to Harvey's party. Perhaps then I'll have another chance. Why can't he get it through his thick skull that we belong together? I don't know how long it's going to take, but he will see it eventually.

Noticing the time, I realize I need to start getting ready for the party. I close my laptop, collect the pages of my sermon from the printer, placing them in my briefcase, and then head upstairs for a shower.

I PULL up to Harvey's house, though it's more of a mansion in my mind. Situated in the prestigious Preston Hollow area, his neighbors are the rich and famous of Dallas. His home sits on three wooded acres.

When I knock on Harvey's door, his boyfriend Nathan answers it.

Nathan is a retired psychologist and close to the same age as Harvey. They were on the cover of our local gay newspaper just last week. The headline of the article read "You're Never Too Old To Find Love."

"Hello, Stephen," Nathan says.

"Hi. Sorry I'm a little late."

"No worries. Come on in. The party is just getting started in the ballroom. Follow me."

As we walk into the expansive room, I notice large photos on the walls. The main subject in every one of them is Malcolm, sometimes alone, sometimes with other people. I see several of my neighbors in some of them, as well as a few men and women I don't recognize in others. It's obvious all the photos and everything else in the space are tributes to him. There are many awards that Malcolm was given on display, including Humanitarian of the Year from the city, Advocate of the Year from our local LGBT organization, and the key to the city he was given after his work with homeless teens, to name just a few.

The room is busting at the seams with people who Malcolm loved and respected and who loved and respected him. Even the mayor is here and several other dignitaries. A photographer from the newspaper is snapping pictures and two TV stations have reporters and camera crews interviewing guests. This is a veritable Who's Who of Dallas. But there is only one *who* I'm interested in finding. *Anthony.*

I scan the room and see some friendly faces near the grand piano but no Anthony. Maybe one of them knows where he is.

I walk over to my neighbors. S & M are talking with LaShaya and Hayden, who live in Unit B. They're the parents of one of the two babies at Mockingbird Place we all love. Since I don't see LaShaya's brother anywhere, I'm certain that Brexton is babysitting, giving them a night out.

Harvey grabs a glass of champagne from one of the server's trays and hands it to me just as I step up. "Glad you could make it."

"Glad to be here. Quite the party you've put together to honor Malcolm." I take a sip. "This is nice."

"It should be, Stephen. It's Dom Pérignon," Oliver says, walking up beside us with his husband, Adam. "Harvey didn't spare any expense."

"And quite the turnout," Adam adds.

Harvey nods. "It's not hard to have a crowd when the honoree is Malcolm."

Chief Torres and his wife walk over to us. He's head of campus security.

"Hey, Chief." Adam is one of his officers.

"Hi, Adam. Oliver." The chief's wife gives them hugs. She kisses Harvey on the cheek. "What a wonderful party. Looks like everyone who loved Malcolm showed up."

"That's the truth," the chief says with a big smile. "I recognize several officers from the Dallas and Fort Worth police and fire departments, and every other city in the Metroplex."

"This would be a good time for a burglar to go on a rampage then," Nathan teases.

"That's true," Chief Torres says.

Harvey smiles. "Please excuse me folks. I need to make an announcement."

As he walks over to a stand with a microphone next to the piano, I glance around the room for Anthony. *No luck.*

He clinks his glass, holding it next to the mike. "May I have your attention for a moment please."

The chatter stops instantly, and everyone turns Harvey's direction.

"As you know we are having this party to celebrate the life of our dear friend, Malcolm Rivers. Today is his birthday. This great man in one way or another has touched each and every one of us. He taught me that one of the most important things in life is to be true to yourself no matter what. It took me a long time to learn that lesson, but I did learn it." Harvey motions to Nathan. "And now I am in love with the most amazing person and having the best time of my life." Harvey lifts his glass and looks up. "Happy birthday, buddy. I miss you." His voice cracks a little as he looks back at all of us. "To Malcolm."

Everyone says, "To Malcolm," and takes a sip of their drink.

"This microphone is for any of you who would like to say a few words about Malcolm and how he influenced your life," Harvey says. "Whenever you feel the urge to share, just step up and tell us your Malcolm story. For now, let's enjoy the music of my favorite band, Red Shimmer."

Two of Red Shimmer's members live in Unit G at Mockingbird Place—Chad and Josh. They are not a couple, but are great friends. The female of the trio, Franki, lives with her fiancée, Candy. I've heard the band a few times, and I'm with Harvey. They are my favorite, too. So talented.

Chad sits at the piano, with Josh and Franki behind him with their guitars.

"This is for you, Malcolm," Chad says.

The trio begins singing their tribute song and the crowd quiets.

As they continue singing, I notice how many of the guests are wiping their eyes. God, I wish I had known him. It's clear that if any man lived their life well, it was Malcolm Rivers. And Harvey is right. Even though Malcolm was already gone when I moved into

Mockingbird Place, I can still feel his influence on me, especially after hearing what Anthony said about him this morning.

Was it just this morning when Anthony knocked on my door? There hasn't been a second since then that I haven't thought about how I could have said something different to keep him from running away from me again. But I just sat there and let him go. I won't make that mistake again. I swear it. I scan the room once again for him, but he's still not here.

When Red Shimmer starts another song, Harvey and Nathan walk over to me.

"Stephen, I want to show something to you and Nathan," Harvey says.

"Okay."

Nathan and I follow him out of the ballroom, down a hall, and up some stairs. When we come to a double door, Harvey leads us inside to his home theater room. It's very plush and can seat comfortably at least fifty people.

"Honey, what's this about?" Nathan asks.

"You and Stephen are the only two people at this event who never met my dear friend Malcolm. With the help of Chad and Oliver, I was able to put several videos together of him especially for you. I feel like once you see them, you'll understand even more why everyone loved him and misses him so much."

Nathan gives him a kiss. "You did this just for Stephen and me?"

He smiles. "I did, though we might use this film for next year's party, if you two don't mind."

"Why would we mind?" I ask. "I'm so honored that you would do this for us."

"Have a seat," he tells Nathan and me.

We sit down and he starts the film.

"I'm going back to the party, guys. I hope you enjoy." Harvey leaves us.

The first images that appear on the screen are of Malcolm and Harvey at a dance.

"They look to be around your age," Nathan says. "My Harvey couldn't be more than twenty-five back then."

"And he is very handsome. Still is."

Nathan smiles and nods.

Two teenage girls appear in frame, whisking a young Malcolm and a young Harvey out to the dance floor.

"Is that S & M?" Nathan asks.

"I believe so," I say. "They're cute, and they can dance too."

The dance fades out and a new image, obviously a few years later, comes into focus. Malcolm is cutting a ribbon for an orphanage in Dallas. The broad smile on his face is evidence at how happy he was to give back.

Each of the following scenes continues taking us through this incredible man's life. His overwhelming generosity and big heart has such an impact on the people that share the screen with him. I can feel the smiles and hugs and happy tears from each and every one of them.

At the next scene change, a much younger Anthony appears in a boxing ring with Malcolm watching from the sidelines. Anthony couldn't be much more than sixteen or seventeen. They are in a gym. Is this the same gym Anthony told me about? Anthony is sparring with a man who is clearly his trainer, and Malcolm is cheering him on. Even back then, Anthony was quite the fighter.

More scenes appear, taking us closer to Malcolm's last days.

The last scene comes into focus. It's a birthday celebration— Malcolm's eightieth birthday. Just a few years before he died. I see Oliver, Eli, Jackson, Trace, S & M, and so many others gathered around him as he blows out the candles on his cake. But the one person I can't stop looking at is standing in the back, as usual. Anthony looks as if he's happy to be there but also looks as if he's feeling out of place. *Anthony, I wish I could help you get rid of your demons.*

When the film stops, I turn to Nathan. "I understand why Harvey did this. I feel as if I really know Malcolm now."

"Me, too," he says. "Shall we go back to the party?"

"Definitely."

When we walk into the ballroom, I spot Anthony on the dance floor with another man. Instantly, jealousy rises up inside me. That's a feeling I don't recall ever experiencing before, and I don't like it.

As Oliver and Adam step next to me, I glare at the guy.

"Who the hell is that with Anthony?" I ask them.

Adam shrugs.

"We don't know," Oliver says. "I asked Nicco if he'd ever seen him before but he also said no."

"Well, I'm going to find out who he is right now." I march over to Anthony and the creep, leaving Oliver and Adam behind.

Why am I so angry and ready for a confrontation? That's not how a priest should be acting, but I don't give a damn. It's how I'm feeling.

I pass Nicco, S & M, and other neighbors, who are standing next to the piano. They are watching the same duo as I am and are clearly confused like me.

The closer I get to Anthony and the other guy, the more I can tell what's going on. Anthony is smashed, something I've never seen before. But what fuels my fury is seeing the bastard groping *my Anthony*.

"Get your hands off of him!"

Anthony turns to me, and I can see his eyes are barely open.

"Stee…pheen," he slurs.

How much did he have to drink? He's on the verge of passing out and clearly isn't aware of what's going on.

"Fuck off, fucker. This is my date, not yours." To prove his point to me, the jerk reaches down and cups Anthony's cock.

"Sorry, Malcolm," I say aloud and reach back into my past talents, hitting the asshole in the face.

The bastard windmills backward several steps before tumbling on his ass.

Anthony stumbles, but I catch him before he falls on his still injured face.

"I'm going to kill you, motherfucker!" The jerk charges me, just as I lay Anthony down.

I slide right, avoiding his attack, and before the man can readjust his maneuver, I pound him with several jabs, finishing him off with a hook and an uppercut. Once again, he lands back down, but this time he's out cold.

The crowd cheers.

My heart is thudding in my chest. I look at Anthony and get down beside him. He's passed out. I hope he's okay. A million questions swirl in my mind. *What were you thinking bringing this guy here? Who is he?*

"Everyone stay put," Harvey announces, holding the microphone, "until Chief Torres and Officer Adam Stockton get this scum out of here."

As Adam and Chief Torres head to the dance floor, I glance and see Jaris and Maddox walking up. Jaris kneels down on the other side of Anthony, and Maddox checks on the guy I just knocked out.

"How is he?" I ask Jaris about Anthony.

He holds Anthony's eyelids open. "I don't know yet, but I do know we need an ambulance."

"Oh, my God." I can't believe this is happening. "Is it alcohol poisoning?"

"No. I think that asshole roofied him."

Once again, rage rolls hot inside me.

"Looks like Father Stephen broke this creep's jaw," Maddox says, clearly impressed and surprised, bringing out his phone. "I'll have the hospital send two ambulances ASAP. One for Anthony and one for this jerk."

I touch Anthony's face. *Please, God. Keep him safe.*

Out of the corner of my eye, I notice Chief Torres and Adam talking to a man I don't recognize. He keeps glancing at me. It's clear that he's with the police, even though he isn't in uniform.

I'm going to be arrested. I can see it all over the news now.

"Local Priest Delivers Quite the Punch." "Priest Arrested at a Preston Hollow Home." "Saint or Sinner? Priest Goes to Jail."

Wait until word of this gets to the bishop. What will my congregation think? I don't care. All I can think about is praying Anthony will be okay.

As the EMTs rush in with gurneys for Anthony and the other guy, Chief Torres and Adam lead the man they were talking with in my direction.

"Father Stephen," the chief says. "This is Detective Derek Stone with the Dallas Police Department."

Though I hate to leave Anthony's side, I stand. "Detective?"

"I'm sorry, Father, but since I saw you throw the first punch, I have no choice. I have to arrest you."

"I know, but I just want to be with Anthony."

"I wish you could. Please put your hands behind your back." He cuffs me and gives me my Miranda rights. "Do you understand each of these rights I have explained to you?"

"Yes." I look at Anthony as the EMTs place him on the gurney. He's still out. *Please God. Please.*

No matter what happens to me, I know I did the right thing. That asshole could have really hurt Anthony. If I had it to do over again, I wouldn't change a thing.

Detective Stone asks, "Having these rights in mind, do you wish to talk to me now?"

"Sure, Detective. Anything you want to ask me I'll answer."

Chapter 7

Detective Stone leads me into the station.

Moments later, a police photographer takes my mug shot and another officer gets my fingerprints.

"I've got some paperwork I need to fill out, Father," Stone says to me. "I'll check on you a little later."

"Would you do me a favor and check on Anthony too? I'd like to know how he's doing."

"Sure thing." Stone leaves, and the officers continue their jobs of getting me processed into their system.

I've been to Lew Sterrett, the county jail, before. Not as a prisoner but as a priest. I've held services here. I thought I knew what the inmates felt, but I had no idea. Not really. It's much harder than I imagined, losing freedom and being accused. This experience is something I never dreamed would happen to me. Well, at least not since seminary.

"Okay, Father," the officer who took my fingerprints says. "Let's go."

He leads me to a holding cell with several other men. Its gray walls and cold steel mirror what I'm feeling. *Please let Anthony be okay.* This is the place I'll wait until my processing is finished.

"Father Stephen?" One of my cellmates takes a seat on the bench next to me. "It is you, isn't it?"

I recognize him as one of the men who have attended my prison services. "Unfortunately, yes. It's me." I study his face, which is round. He's a little overweight but has kind eyes. "You're…Sam, right?"

He smiles. "That's me. I'm surprised you remembered. It's been at least three months since I was in here last."

"What happened to land you back here, Sam?"

"Too much to drink again. I mouthed off to a bartender when he refused to sell me another beer. Let's just say the rest is history." He narrows his eyes. "What about you? Why are you on this side of the bars?"

"Let's just say there was a meeting of my fists and a jerk's face."

"Father? A man of the cloth?"

"Someone I care a great deal about was in trouble." I can feel my insides tightening as I think about that man groping Anthony, who the bastard had drugged. "I wasn't about to turn the other cheek."

"Huh. I always thought priests weren't capable of such things."

"Sam, I may be a priest but I'm still flesh and blood, just like you."

"Yes, you definitely are." He smiles. "Sounds like something I would have done…especially for someone I loved. Good for you. I'm sure you won't be in here long."

I hope he's right. I want to get to the hospital as soon as I can to check on Anthony. Even though I'm supposed to deliver the sermon in the morning, I doubt I'll be able to. Despite Sam's optimism, I'll probably still be in jail. I know for a fact that it can take several hours to get through the system and make bail. I'll give it a little more time before I ask to call someone to fill in for me. Who knows? Maybe Sam is right and I'll get out quickly.

Two more men join us in the cell. I'm anxious to hear how Anthony is doing. Where is Stone? He promised to come back and tell me about Anthony's condition.

"I know what will cheer you up," Sam says, clearly sensing my inner turmoil. "This song always works for me."

He starts humming "When the Saints Go Marching In."

The next thing I know, two of the guys closest to us begin singing the song.

"Oh, when the saints go marching in. Oh, when the saints go marching in. Lord I want to be in that number, when the saints go marching in."

More men begin singing along.

"Come on, Father," Sam says with a big grin. "Join in."

I nod and start singing with our makeshift choir. The weight begins to lift from me ever so slightly with each chorus and verse. Before long, nearly every man in the cell is either singing loudly, humming along, clapping hands, or tapping feet.

Sam leans over to me. "Now this is what I call church, Father."

Detective Stone walks into our cell and motions to me.

I stand and step next to him.

He looks at me and smiles as the choir continues. "This is your doing, no doubt."

"Actually, it was Sam's doing." I point out the man who lifted everyone's spirit.

"Oh, Reverend Sam," Stone says.

"Reverend?"

Stone nods. "Sam is an ordained Pentecostal minister."

"I didn't know that." I glance back at Sam, once again reminded that you can't judge a book by its cover. "Do you know what happened to Sam?"

"A tornado killed his wife and infant son in West Texas. That's when he started drinking. But every time he's in here he always encourages the other inmates."

Waving good-bye to Sam as we exit the cell, I vow to myself that I'm going to find a way to help this special man of God. "What about Anthony? How is he?"

"The hospital staff wouldn't tell me anything since I'm not a relative. I tried to reach Harvey but keep getting his voicemail. The likely reason is that the reception at the hospital is very poor. The good news is you made bail, so you can go check for yourself."

When I see Father Grissom waiting for us in the hallway, I know the dear man is the one who posted bail for me. Despite our age difference, nearly four decades, I couldn't ask for a better friend than him. But he's more than just a friend to me. He's a mentor to me. A counselor. Someone I can always depend on.

I place my hand on his shoulder. "Thank you, Father."

"You're welcome, Stephen."

"Who told you I was arrested?"

"Harvey. He also told me everything else that happened. Let's get you to the hospital. I'm sure you're very anxious to check on Anthony."

A LITTLE PAST five in the morning, Father Grissom and I run into the waiting room and find S & M, Nicco, Harvey and Nathan, and other Mockingbird neighbors.

"Any news yet?" I ask them, hearing the panic in my tone.

"No. We don't know anything about Anthony or that bastard." Nicco stands, as do the rest of my friends.

They surround me, wrapping me in their collective arms.

"We're so glad you're out," Sarah says.

Martha kisses me on the cheek. "What a nightmare."

"Would you like some coffee?" Harvey asks. "I brought a thermos. You know how bad hospital coffee is."

"What do you mean bad coffee?" Martha smiles. "I know for a fact that this hospital has drip coffee that is fantastic."

Harvey shrugs. "Maybe so, but it's still not as good as mine. What do you say, Stephen? Would you like a cup?"

"No, thanks. I just want to hear that Anthony is okay."

Wearing his scrubs, Jaris walks into the room. "He's stable. The blood test revealed that he received a lethal dose of gamma hydroxybutyrate."

Nicco looks stunned. "That sonofabitch gave him a date rape drug?"

Jaris nods. "GHB is a central nervous system depressant. Just 5ccs mixed with alcohol can render a person unconscious and severely impact respiration, and Anthony was slipped a lot more than 5ccs." He looks at me. "It's a good thing that you did what you did, Stephen. If you hadn't, it might have been too late. He's going to be fine, but we have to keep him a few days to make sure the drug is completely out of his bloodstream."

Even though I'm relieved that Anthony is okay, I'm still anxious to find out for myself. "When can we see him, Doc?"

"He's conscious but he's still a little disoriented. He needs to rest."

Seeing Martha lean forward, I know that she isn't going to give up that easy.

"Jaris, you know how S and I feel when someone we love is in the hospital."

"Of course, I know. It's the Mockingbird Place way to have at least one person stay with them."

"Doc, I'd like to stay with him first," Nicco says. "I'll be quiet."

"Okay. Um…let's do this. Stephen, you can go in with Nicco, but only for five minutes. The rest of you, I'd prefer you wait until in the morning to see him. Deal?"

Knowing I'm not a relative, I look at S & M to see their reaction.

They both wink at me and in unison answer, "Deal."

Sarah continues, "But we're not going home until Stephen and Nicco get back and give us their report."

Nicco and I follow Jaris. As we pass through doors marked "Intensive Care Unit" I realize how very serious this is for Anthony. *Please God. Please.*

We walk into Anthony's room. His eyes are closed. He's hooked up to monitors, has an IV attached to the back of his left hand, and is receiving oxygen in his nose. Seeing him like this, I feel the blood drain out of me.

"Five minutes, guys. No more." Jaris leaves us alone with Anthony.

"That fucker." Nicco's words sound more like a growl than language. "He'll pay for what he did to my brother."

"You'll have to stand in line behind me."

"A priest can't do that, Father."

"Watch me."

"Hey, bro." Anthony's voice is very weak. "Where am I? What am I doing? Did I win the fight with O'Brien?" Before Nicco or I can answer, Anthony looks at me and smiles. "Oh. My sweetheart. You're here, Stephen. You're really here."

I realize it must be the drugs talking and not Anthony. "Yes. I'm here."

"I love you."

I feel my legs weaken. Those three words I've longed to hear from him for so long. But I can't believe they're real under these circumstances.

His eyes close. "Are you still here, Stephen?"

"Yes, Anthony. I'm still here."

He mumbles something that neither Nicco or I can make out. I lean in close, placing my ear next to his lips. "What did you say?"

Anthony's next three breathy words brush against my skin and utterly melt me to my core.

"Please kiss me."

Chapter 8

I close the hospital door to Anthony's room and lean against the wall.

God, I really wanted to kiss him. So much. But I couldn't, not with him drugged up. It wouldn't have been right. *Or real.*

Still, my mind keeps replaying his words over and over. "I love you. Please kiss me."

There's nothing more I want to do than comfort him. But I can't.

He could have died.

That thought shakes me to my core. I can't imagine a world without him in it, and yet there's not a thing I can do. Jaris says he's going to be okay. Thank God.

I look at the clock on my cell. I've got plenty of time before the church service starts. Looks like I'll be able to deliver that sermon after all.

Just as one of Anthony's nurses walks in, Nicco comes out.

As the door closes once again, Nicco places his hand on my shoulder. "I know that must have been tough for you."

"It was. Very."

"You love my brother, don't you?"

I look him straight in the eyes. "With all my heart."

He smiles. "I knew it. This is great news. You are exactly the kind of man I want for him."

"Maybe so, but Anthony is afraid to be with me."

Nicco nods. "He's afraid to open up to me or S & M. And you? He's terrified of you because when he's around you his walls start to crumble. What happened to him when he was so young scarred Tony, and he's afraid to trust anyone."

"I know. That's why I didn't kiss him." I take a deep breath. "But I will not give up, Nicco. I do love your brother."

"And you saved his life. Jaris said so." Nicco wraps his arms around me, which may seem odd to some given how tough he is.

He doesn't say a word for several seconds, but keeps holding onto me. It's clear how much he cares about Anthony. Nicco is living proof of what it really means to be your brother's keeper.

"Thank you." He steps back, trying to keep me from seeing him wipe his eyes. "We need to get back to the others to let them know how Anthony is doing."

Nicco may be a tough guy, but he's got a huge heart.

We walk into the waiting room.

S & M rush up to us.

Martha looks at Nicco and me. "How is he?"

"He's good but still very out of it," Nicco answers. "It's going to take a while."

I notice S & M's eyes are welling up so I give them a hug. "He's in very good hands. I'm sure when you come in the morning he'll be more awake."

Detective Stone walks in from the hallway. "Father Norelli, I thought I would find you here."

S & M and Nicco step in front of me, as if to create a protective wall.

"Why are you here, Detective?" Sarah asks in a firm tone. "Stephen made bail."

Before he can answer, Chief Torres and Adam enter.

"Oh, good," Adam says. "You're all here."

"Yes, we're here, and it better be good." Martha's tone is just as firm as her wife's.

Detective Stone smiles. "I haven't had a chance to tell them yet. But as you can see for yourself, these three circled their wagons around Father Stephen when I came in."

Adam and the chief start laughing.

"This isn't a laughing matter, young men." Sarah's scolding is always done in love. "One of you needs to tell us what's going on, and you need to do it right now."

I step around my self-declared protectors. "It's okay. Let's hear what they have to say. Detective?"

"Good news. I just spoke with the DA. You've been exonerated, Father Stephen, for all charges brought against you. The man in question, whose jaw you broke, drugged Anthony Mantonvani and nearly took his life. Without your intervention, according to the attending physicians, Mr. Mantonvani would have likely died."

I'm stunned but grateful.

"Stephen, we must have a celebration for you." Martha claps her hands together. Her exuberance is very contagious. "S and I have peach cobbler, apple pie, chocolate cake, and ice cream."

"And M and I will stop at the grocery store and get a fruit and veggie plate for those, like me, who are watching their calories."

"Why don't we cook some burgers and hot dogs?" Martha asks.

Sarah kisses her on the cheek. "That's why I love you so much. Beautiful and brilliant."

"I love you, too." Martha brings out her phone. "I'll text everyone to meet us at our apartment after Stephen's church services."

Sarah leans forward. "What do you say to that, Fath…I mean Stephen?"

"Don't you think this is too much trouble? I actually broke the man's jaw."

"And rightly so," Nicco says.

"Stephen, you haven't lived at Mockingbird Place long, but you'll learn that M and I love hosting parties for our friends."

"Then there's only one thing for me to say. Sounds delicious."

She turns to Adam and Chief Torres. "I expect you and your spouses there too."

Adam salutes her. "Yes, ma'am."

Chief Torres nods. "Me and my wife will be there."

She looks at Detective Stone. "And you will be coming too."

He smiles. "Sure."

"And bring your significant other, if you have one."

"He has one," the chief says. "Titus Love, the best tattoo artist in the city."

"Thanks for the invitation," Stone says. "Titus and I will definitely be there. Can we bring something?"

Martha grins. "You and Titus and everyone else only need to bring a healthy appetite."

"I'll stay here with Tony," Nicco says.

"You are a wonderful brother." Martha kisses him on the cheek. "We'll bring you a plate."

"After the celebration, I'll come back to the hospital to help," I tell him.

Sarah kisses me on the cheek. "You're wonderful too, Stephen. One of us needs to be with Anthony until he comes home. We can all take turns."

"I like that plan." Nicco shakes my hand. "I'm going back to Anthony's room."

THE HOT SHOWER helps relieve my tight muscles. I look at my left hand, which is still swollen from punching that jerk. I grin. *God, forgive me for calling him a jerk.*

The last twenty-four hours have been some of the most difficult of my life. Thank goodness, it's Sunday. As much as I'd like to be at the hospital, the people at my church are counting on me. The good thing is I always find comfort at church, and I could really use some comfort now.

As I dry off, I wonder how I am going to be able to deliver my sermon with so much on my mind. I wipe off the moisture on the mirror and look at my face.

Dressing quickly, I put on my white collar and take one last look at myself in the mirror.

"Malcolm deserves your best, as do all your parishioners." I sigh, wondering how Anthony is doing. I'm so glad that Nicco is with him. I certainly won't worry as much knowing he's there. He promised he would call me if there were any changes.

I PULL into my parking spot. Usually, I'm one of the first to arrive. Not today. The lot is full, and the service is supposed to start very soon.

The Episcopal Church of the Beloved Disciple is a little white church with a steeple, which most would expect to see in the country, not a major urban city like Dallas. It sits amidst tall elm trees that create a beautiful canopy that is very soothing. Next year is the church's fiftieth anniversary, and the vestry is making lots of plans to celebrate. I'm still amazed that I'm the rector, the youngest in the diocese. I became rector here a few months ago, and I'm enjoying having my own church.

I walk through the door. Before I can duck into the sacristy to put on vestments, Mrs. Clark, who is on the vestry, stops me. Even though she's a little over five feet tall and just shy of ninety years old, Mrs. Clark is definitely not a pushover. She's been one of my biggest supporters since I became rector, and she's made sure everyone else in the parish supports me too. If not, they would have to deal with her wrath, and no one wants to do that. We all adore her.

"Father Stephen, I'm so glad you're here." Her Texas accent is so cute. "I wasn't sure you would make it."

"Sorry, I'm late."

"We were all so worried about you getting arrested."

So much for keeping it a secret. "You know about that?"

"Of course I do. You remember that the mayor is a friend of

mine, as is the chief of police. They were at Harvey's party to honor Malcolm." She sighs. "Malcolm was such a dear man. He and I served on the vestry many times over the years. I was supposed to come to the party, but I had one of my sinking spells. You know how that goes." She smiles. "I guess you don't. You're too young to know about such things. Anyway, I was so concerned when the mayor and chief called to let me know that you might not be here today because you punched that wicked man in the face. I'm so glad they were wrong."

"Me, too."

She leans in close, concern in her eyes. "How's Anthony?"

"He'll be fine."

"That's very good news. I'm sure you're relieved." She hugs me, making me wonder how much more she knows about me. Nothing would surprise me when it comes to Mrs. Clark.

We hear the organist start to play.

"That's my cue, Mrs. Clark." I hug her. "I have to hurry and get in my vestments, but I will make an announcement for everyone so they won't be worried."

After I finish getting ready, I step next to the acolytes just in time to begin the procession to the altar. I see the regular members in the pews, and also some of my neighbors.

Harvey and Nathan are sitting next to Oliver and Adam. Behind them are LaShaya and her husband Hayden with their baby. Her brother Brexton sits by S & M. Even Chad is here, and all the rest of my Mockingbird Place family. Only Nicco and Anthony are missing.

They're clearly here to give me their support, and I definitely need it.

At the appropriate time in the service, I step up to the lectern. "Before I begin my sermon, I would like to inform you of what happened last night to me. Some of you may already know that I was privileged to enjoy the Dallas County Correctional facilities."

I hear a few chuckles and some gasps.

"Yes, your rector was arrested and went to jail." As best and succinctly as I can, I tell them what happened. "The good news is all the charges have been exonerated. The bad news is…" I hold up my left hand so everyone can see. "My fist is still swollen."

The crowd erupts in laughter, which puts me at ease.

"I bet the other guy's face looks a lot worse," one of the older men shout. "That's the way we handled bullies back in my day, Father Stephen."

More laughter follows.

Once everyone quiets, I begin the sermon. "The story of the Good Samaritan is one most of us are very familiar with. It teaches us that we should love God and our neighbors. But more importantly, it defines who our neighbors are. Who saw the man who had been attacked, robbed, and left to die? Three men, but only one really saw him. Not the priest or the religious man. They avoided getting involved. They had places to go, people to see, important matters to deal with. But the last man, a stranger, didn't look away. His heart was touched and he gave him first aid. But he didn't stop there. No. He took him to an inn, made him comfortable. Opened his purse strings and paid the bill, and told the innkeeper if the man needed more he would be back to pay the rest.

"One man, who was a member of this church since its founding nearly fifty years ago, lived his life like the Good Samaritan. Malcolm Rivers. Regretfully, I never met him, but I know a few of the people he helped." I continue the sermon with how Malcolm rescued Anthony from the streets.

I see S & M and many others wiping the tears from their eyes. "I'm lucky to have many examples of Good Samaritans…good neighbors…around me. I want to be a better—"

My phone rings and I jump.

"Sorry. I meant to put that on silent."

A few chuckles make me smile.

Nicco's name is on my caller ID. "This is Anthony's brother, folks. Let me find out how he's doing. Hello, Nicco? Is he okay?"

"He is doing much better. The drugs are wearing off. He's awake and wants to see you."

Chapter 9

After church, I rush to my car, anxious to get to Anthony. Less than five blocks later, I see red and blue lights flashing in my rearview mirror. *God, I know you're busy today since it's Sunday, but I really could use a break, if you don't mind.*

As the officer approaches, I wonder if I'm going to keep getting in trouble with the police. Sure seems like things are turning out that way of late. Of course, I was speeding.

I roll down my window. "Hello, Officer."

He's a big man, at least six-foot-four. The nameplate on his uniform reads "Winslow."

I'm glad that our police department has men like him to keep the peace. After the tragic mass shooting of cops in July, the city has really pulled together.

His eyes widen slightly when he sees my collar. "Father. May I see your license and insurance?"

"Of course." I hand them to him.

He looks them over and gives them back to me. "Father Norelli, where are you headed to so fast today?"

"The hospital."

"Oh. I'll give you an escort the rest of the way since I've held you up." As he walks away, he says, "Turn on your flashers so everyone will know you're with me."

Before I can tell him it's not an emergency, he's already in his car pulling out with lights still flashing.

I'm embarrassed, but I have no choice. I have to follow him. And besides, I will get to the hospital quicker. Maybe this is God's way of giving me a break.

We pull up to the ER entrance, and I park in one of the clergy spots.

The officer rolls down his window. "Sorry I stopped you, Father. I wish I had known it was an emergency."

Priests aren't supposed to lie, Stephen. "It really isn't an emergency, but it's important to me."

"Well, if it's important to you than it's important to me." He smiles and points to the sky. "Put in a good word for Officer Dale Winslow with your boss."

"I definitely will. Thank you, Officer."

As he drives away, I make a mental note to mention his name to the chief of police.

I rush into the hospital with Nicco's words ringing in my ears.

"He's awake and wants to see you."

When I enter Anthony's hospital room, I'm thrilled to see him sitting up in bed, eating a sandwich and drinking a glass of milk.

In the chair next to him is Nicco, who looks up from his magazine. "Stephen."

Seeing me, Anthony stretches out his arms to me. "Come here and give me a hug."

Before I can move next to the bed, Nicco stands. "I'm glad you're here. I'd like to grab a bite from the cafeteria."

"Of course," I say, though I'm not sure it's the best idea for me to be alone with Anthony right now. I almost blew it and kissed him the last time I was here.

"So go, Nicco." Anthony points at the door. "I'd like a little private time with Stephen."

"Oh, you do, do you? Okay. I'll be back shortly." He grins, winks at me, and leaves.

Nicco is once again letting it be very clear that he wants Anthony and I together. His strong approval is making it difficult for me to resist Anthony. Still, I know that's the right thing to do.

"So, handsome. Are you going to just stand in the doorway staring at me or are you going to give me a hug like I asked?"

Even though my heart is breaking and everything inside me wants to hold Anthony and never let go, I walk over to him, silently reminding myself that he's still under the influence of the drugs. *I don't know how much more of this I can take.*

I look at him. "Hey."

He grabs me, pulls me down, and gives me the best hug I've ever had. I can't help myself and hug him back. It feels so good to have him in my arms, no matter what the circumstances. I know I'm crossing the line a little, but I haven't jumped all the way over it. I just love him so much.

Anthony turns his head until our eyes lock.

Do the right thing, Stephen.

Before I can let go of him, he lightly touches his lips to my cheek, causing my strength and resolve to weaken.

"Anthony, we shouldn't—"

His kiss silences me. He presses his lips tighter to mine, and God help me, I know I've gone way past the line.

And far beyond.

"Oh. I didn't mean to interrupt." Jaris's words jar me. "I can come back."

I step away from Anthony and turn around to face Jaris in his white coat with a stethoscope around his neck. "No. Uh. It's okay. Umm. I…we…well, you're the doctor."

Jaris grins. "Yes, I am."

"Stephen, you're not going, are you?" Anthony's sexy voice is a force of nature to me, like everything else about him.

Even though leaving would be better for both of us, I promised Nicco I would stay until he got back. "Of course, I'm staying. I want to hear what Jaris has to say."

Guilt claws at my insides. How could I have been so stupid? I knew better. If Jaris hadn't showed up when he did, I would have just kept on kissing Anthony. I don't want him to hate me once all the drugs are out of his system.

I step as far away from the bed as I can, hoping that the distance will clear my head and help me get back to the other side of the line I crossed.

"How are you feeling, Tony?" Jaris glances at the monitor showing Anthony's chart.

"Really good. When can I go home?"

"Let me get a better look at you first, before I answer that." Jaris studies Anthony's pupils. "Still dilated but much better. According to your last blood test, the drugs are still in your system, but the numbers are lower now. So by tomorrow you probably can go home."

"By the way, Doc, how is O'Brien?"

"He was released this morning. Which reminds me." Jaris reaches into his pocket and pulls out a slip of paper. He hands it to him. "He asked me to give this to you."

I watch Anthony look at the note.

"Stephen, come closer and read this to me." He smiles. "My eyes aren't focusing very well."

I'm pretty sure that he just wants me near him. Maybe I should stay put. The space between me and Anthony, though only a few steps, has helped me settle down. Still, I am curious to hear what O'Brien had to say, so I move back next to the bed.

Anthony hands me the note.

I read it aloud. "'Hey, Mantonvani. Got word from Joe that you were in here too. I'm getting released, but I can't wait to get back in the cage with you. Get well, my friend.' It is signed just 'O'Brien.'"

Anthony grins. "That guy doesn't know when to give up. I'm clearly the better fighter. Besides, I like him too much to fight him again. I'd be in there throwing it for him, and then I'd end up in trouble."

"Like that would ever happen." Jaris laughs. "I've been to many of your fights. You let your opponents wail on you at the beginning, but then the ferocity that emerges from you always gets you the win. No matter what you say, I know you will never sandbag a match even against a friend." He looks at me. "I am right, aren't I, Stephen?"

"Of course you are, Doc."

"Of course you are, Doc." Anthony bursts out laughing. "Get it, Stephen? I said exactly what you said."

"I get it." I grin. *You're still on drugs, all right.*

"You do get me." Anthony grabs my hand. "More than anyone else."

Not wanting to make a scene or upset him, I don't pull away. I just let him hold my hand, and I have to admit I'm enjoying it.

I glance at Jaris and realize I'm not the only one to have noticed how Anthony acts in a fight, holding back until his opponent's punches push him to the very edge. Has Jaris also seen him whisper into each fighter's ear just before he pounds them to the mat?

I remember O'Brien telling me what Anthony whispered to him before he punched him into oblivion.

"You'll never hurt me again, you fucking pedophile."

Those words tell me so much about the pain Anthony lives with every day.

Dear God, help me to help him.

Nicco walks back into the room and glances at me holding hands with Anthony. "Hey, Doc. How's my little brother?"

"I'm great, Nicco," Anthony answers before Jaris can answer. "I got my man here with me. He's good medicine."

I release Anthony's hand, feeling mixed emotions. As much as I wish this shortcut could be real, I know it isn't. Once the drugs are completely out of his system his walls are going to come right back. I know it. Even so, I will not give up. Whatever it takes to break through his boundaries, I will do. Brick by brick. I love him, and I know he loves me too, even if he's not ready to admit it without the drugs.

Jaris tells him about Anthony's condition. "He'll be ready to go home in the morning."

"That's great, Doc," Nicco says and turns to me. "I guess you are good medicine for my brother."

"I certainly hope so, but I really have to go. I'm already late for S & M's celebration for me getting out of jail."

"Jail? You were in jail?" Anthony's face shows concern. "What for?"

Damn it, Stephen. You need to learn to keep your mouth shut. "Uhh…it doesn't matter."

Nicco's eyes narrow. "Oh, yes, it does matter. You saved my brother's life."

Anthony is still confused. "Saved my life? What the hell are you talking about? I don't even know why I'm in the hospital now that I think about it."

Nicco is clearly troubled because of Anthony's memory lapse. "But I told you. Don't you remember?"

"Nicco, that's not unusual," Jaris says. "Don't worry. The drugs are wearing off."

I look into Anthony's eyes, noticing his pupils look more normal. It's a good thing that the roofie is leaving his system, but as it weakens, he's becoming more and more agitated. Who wouldn't be in his circumstances?

"Anthony, what do you remember about last night?" I ask.

"Nothing. Absolutely nothing. Will somebody tell me what's going on?"

"Just calm down. We'll tell you everything." Jaris's words, though typical for any doctor, are really coming from his heart. Anthony is not just his patient. He's his friend.

"Anthony, what's the last thing you remember?" I ask.

He takes a deep breath. "Give me a minute." He closes his eyes. "I was sitting in a bar on Cedar Springs having a beer before Harvey's party. This guy walked up to me. He introduced himself… and uh…we were talking. What was his name?"

"Was it Russell Evans?" Jaris asks.

He opens his eyes. "I think so. Yes. I remember. His name *was* Russell. That's it. A really good-looking guy and very nice. Bought me a drink."

A really good-looking guy? And very nice? I can feel jealousy rising up inside me. And I'm angry. I am really angry.

"And then…uh…I don't know. I woke up here."

"Damn it, Anthony. You almost died. Why did you put yourself in such a dangerous situation?"

"Because I was mad at you," he answers. "Really mad at you. I needed to get my mind on something else."

"I know you were, but what the hell did I do to you?"

"You told me you loved me, that's what."

"That made you so mad that you ran to another man's arms?"

"He was a stranger to me. I didn't care anything about him."

"And you don't care anything about me either, do you?"

He doesn't say anything. His walls are back up.

"I love you. That's the truth. *My* truth. When you're ready to tell me *your* truth, you know where I live."

Marching past Nicco and Jaris, who I'd actually forgotten were still here, I say, "Sorry, guys."

Even though my heart is breaking, I still leave Anthony's room. *Please God. I need him. Help me.*

Chapter 10

Though I'm not really in the mood for a party, especially after what happened at the hospital between Anthony and me, I'm hoping my friends will give me a lift. When I walk into S & M's apartment, Unit I, I'm stunned to see all the decorations commemorating my release from jail. There's a huge "Get Out Of Jail Free" card hanging near the stairs. S & M are wearing prisoner outfits. Plastic handcuffs and police batons are on every table.

"Hey, everyone," Sarah yells. "The jailbird is free, and he's here."

They all turn my direction and shout, "Congratulations!"

"Thank you."

Each holding their baby, LaShaya and Ava scoot next to me.

"Ava and I baked a cake for you, but you don't need it now," LaShaya says with a grin.

Ava places a small cake on the coffee table. "But you never know if he might need it later."

"I don't understand," I say.

She hands me a fork. "Just take a bite. You'll see."

"Okay." Once I stick the fork inside and feel it hit against something metal, all my confusion vanishes. "Don't tell me there's a file inside."

"Okay," LaShaya says with a grin. "We won't."

I burst out laughing as I pull out the file, holding it up for everyone to see.

The crowd laughs with me, but then they start bombarding me with lots of questions about Anthony.

Ava leans forward. "First, has Anthony been able to eat anything yet?"

"Stephen, does Jaris think all the drugs are out of his blood stream?" LaShaya asks.

"Is he going to get out today?" Harvey hands me a glass of champagne.

More questions are asked by others before Martha raises her hands. "Hold on, everybody. Stephen just got here. One at a time. Me first."

The crowd quiets.

She smiles and then turns back to me. "How are *you* doing?"

"Glad to be out of jail. Under the circumstances, I'm doing okay. Here's the update, everyone. Anthony is doing fine. I was just with him and he was eating a sandwich and drinking milk. His vitals are great. Jaris says that after one final blood test to make absolutely sure the drugs are out of his system, he should be released tomorrow."

"That's wonderful news." Martha's tone is full of relief.

Sarah hugs her. "It sure is, sweetheart. It sure is. Everyone lift your glass, for Anthony and Stephen. They've both been through a lot. Cheers!"

"Cheers," everyone says in unison.

I was right. My friends are lifting my spirits.

I spot Father Grissom standing next to Oliver and Adam in the dining room. He waves me over. I hope I can get a chance to talk to him in private.

He smiles. "Hello, Stephen. Fantastic sermon this morning."

"It sure was," Adam says

"I wish Malcolm could have heard it. You honored him perfectly." Oliver's voice cracks, and Adam puts his arm around him. "It was like you had actually met him."

"I feel like I have in a way, Oliver. Hearing everyone's stories about him and seeing Harvey's videos brought him to life for me. I know I would have loved the man."

"And he would have loved you," Oliver says.

"All right, everyone. It's time to serve lunch," Martha announces, making me realize they held off serving the meal until I arrived. "S & I have asked Father Grissom to say the blessing. Bow your heads and close your eyes."

Her take-charge attitude always makes me smile.

Not only does Father Grissom bless the food, but he also says some wonderful words about me. "We're all so glad that Father Stephen won't be wearing orange. Everyone knows he's a winter and orange washes him out. Amen."

The crowd laughs, and a few give "Amen" responses.

When things die down here, I'm going to ask Father Grissom to come over to my place. I really need someone to talk to about what happened with Anthony.

"Let's eat," Sarah says.

The spread she and Martha put together for this party is impressive. Hot dogs, hamburgers, potato salad, baked beans, and several desserts.

As everyone lines up to fill their plates, Father Grissom asks me, "How did those two wonderful women put this together so quickly?"

"You're looking at two real live miracle workers," I say. "I have no clue how they do it, but they always manage."

"You are very lucky to have such good friends, Stephen." Father Grissom grabs us both plates and hands one to me.

"I know I am. It wasn't always so for me." I look around the room and am filled with gratitude. "Moving to Mockingbird Place is one of the best things that has happened to me."

"I've got my eyes on a piece of that chocolate cake," he says. "I hope there's some left after I finish this plate."

"If I know S & M, there is at least one backup cake somewhere. Maybe two."

After a couple of hours of enjoying the delicious food and visiting with everyone, the crowd thins out.

I turn to Martha. "Let me help clean up."

"Me, too," Father Grissom adds. "I'm quite the master at washing dishes."

"This party was for you, Stephen. The man of honor doesn't clean up. And Father, you are our guest. Besides, it won't take S and me very long. After all, we used paper plates."

"We just happen to have a bottle of wine that we've been dying to open," Sarah says. "Would you gentlemen join us for a drink?"

"I'd love too," Father Grissom says.

"I would love too as well."

The four of us sit down and enjoy the wine.

"Thank you so much for the party," I say to S & M. "You don't know how much it means to me. I've never had a party in my honor before."

"Not even a birthday party?" Martha asks.

"Nope. I was in foster care most of my childhood."

"Oh my goodness, Stephen." Sarah looks at me with the sweetest eyes. "We never knew that."

"It's not something I talk about much."

"But maybe you should," Father Grissom says, turning to S & M. "He's told me some of his story, since I've become a kind of mentor to him, but not everything."

"Stephen, you are very dear to us," Martha says. "It breaks my heart to learn you never had a party until today. Believe you me, you're going to have a lot of parties from now on."

"You need to talk to us, young man," Sarah says in a motherly tone. "What was your childhood like? Did something happen to your parents?"

"No, they were just extremely young. Only thirteen and fourteen years old."

"Oh, my God." Martha's eyes widen. "They were just babies themselves."

"The way I understand it, they wanted to keep me but their parents wouldn't let them. I ended up in the system."

"Were you adopted?" Sarah asks. "Aren't newborns usually adopted?"

"That's what they tell me, but I had cancer."

Hers and Martha's eyes are welling up. "A baby having cancer. How horrible."

"The doctors got all of it. And look, I'm still here," I add, hoping to ease their concern. "I don't remember any of it. Still, everyone was scared to adopt me. By the time I was through with all the surgeries and treatments, I was two years old. From then on I was in foster care. The foster parents I remember were John and Louise. They kept several children like me. They believed in the old saying 'spare the rod and spoil the child,' and I had many bruises on my legs and back to prove it. We all did. I was five when CPS found out and took us all away."

I pause, thinking I'm over-sharing with them.

The three of them don't say a word. They clearly know how hard this is for me.

Maybe I should just end my story here. But isn't that what Anthony does? He lets people get a little peek at his truth and then the walls come back up and he runs away.

I don't want him to do that anymore, so I won't do it now.

"CPS didn't have enough foster parents back then to take all of us. Me and one other boy ended up in an orphanage. Tommy was lucky and was adopted a month later, leaving me alone. The staff at the orphanage wasn't mean to me or the other children. There just wasn't any love. They were all business. I had clean clothes, a place to sleep, and three meals a day." I sigh. "There just wasn't any love. I'm sorry. I'm repeating myself."

Sarah grabs my hand. "I wish M and I had known you back then. We would have adopted you, but it's never too late to give you love."

"Now go on," Martha says. "We need to hear the whole story. You're ours now, Stephen. Tell us everything."

I feel my eyes welling up. "I had a chip on my shoulder and

treated the staff and other children terribly. No one knew what to do with me. It wasn't just being an orphan that fueled my anger. I was struggling with being gay. When I turned thirteen, a new volunteer came in who changed my life. He was an Episcopal priest. Father O'Malley. Best basketball player I'd ever seen. Whatever rebellion or sarcastic comment I threw at him, he just smiled and kept dribbling that damn ball. I refused to play with him and the other boys. Months went by like that, but I began to give in to his gentle patience.

"Sounds like O'Malley is a helluva priest," Father Grissom says.

"He sure was to me. I told you I never had a party, which is true. But I did get a birthday present. My first one ever. *From him.* I turned fourteen and he walked into the orphanage with three tickets to see the Dallas Mavericks. One for him. One for me. And one for his wife. The Mavs won. After the game they took me to a nice restaurant. His wife was so sweet. They asked me so many questions. For the first time in my life I felt completely at ease and answered all of them. The final question was the best. They asked me if I would like to be their son. With all my heart I wanted to say yes, but I couldn't. I was afraid that if they found out I was gay they wouldn't want me. I just sat there silent."

My mind brings up that night as clear as if it were yesterday.

FATHER O'MALLEY ASKS, "What's the matter?"

I lie. "Nothing is the matter."

He places his hand on my shoulder. "Are you worried because you're gay?"

"How do you know that?" I look at him, feeling exposed, like he can see everything about me.

"When you love someone as much as Ellen and I love you, you sense things about them. About you. I just know, son. Because I love you."

She grabs my hand. "Gay or straight or whatever, Stephen, we want you in our family."

"But what about God?" I turn to him. "You're a priest. You can't have a gay son. Won't God be mad at you? Isn't it a sin?"

"There are some that believe it is, but I'm not one of them. God made all of us. We're all different, each in our own special way."

"That's right, honey," she says. *"I'm left handed. Centuries ago, some believed people like me were very bad. That's no longer the case. And Stephen, I believe in time that more people will come to see that love is love. No matter what. You're a child of God, Stephen. Believe that."*

I TAKE a sip of wine and look at the three people around me. They love me and I love them.

"You know what my answer was after that?"

"You said 'yes,' right?" Sarah asks.

"No. I said, 'You've got to be kidding. You still want to adopt me?'" I grin, remembering that wonderful moment. "When I realized they meant it, I jumped out of my chair and hugged them. Then I said yes over and over with tears rolling down my cheeks. They told me that they would meet with their attorney the next day to get the ball rolling. Father O'Malley said that as soon as it was legal, they would be moving me into their home. That was the greatest day of my life. But I never got adopted."

"What happened to change their mind, sweetheart?" Martha asks.

"Nothing changed their mind. They were on their way home after seeing their attorney about the adoption. A man who had robbed a store moments earlier blasted past a red light just as Father O'Malley pulled his and his wife's car into the intersection. They were killed instantly and the robber died a few hours later."

Sarah wipes her eyes. "Oh, my poor baby. How horrible."

"It was, but for the first time in my life I had felt real love. Not only had they got the adoption papers put together with their attorney that day, they also redid their will, leaving everything to me. They weren't rich but I was able to pay for all my college tuition because of them." I pull out my phone and show them the picture of Father O'Malley, his wife, and me at that restaurant. "I still miss them so much. With the orphanage staff's permission, I started attending the church where he'd been the rector. I found peace and meaning. I remained in the orphanage, helping other troubled boys, until I turned eighteen. I was forever changed. I wasn't angry anymore. I wanted to help others. That's why I became a priest."

"I'm sure they would be so proud of you." Father Grissom refills our glasses. "I'd like to offer a toast to the memory of Father O'Malley and his wife, Ellen. May we all be as kind and loving to children as those two dear people were to our Stephen."

"Amen," S & M say together.

"I was thinking of talking with Father Grissom alone about what happened with Anthony and me today, but now I would like to include you. You're very wise."

"Yes, we are," Sarah says with a wink. "And we got the years to prove it."

I smile. "Plus, you know Anthony better than anyone."

"Yes, we do." Martha kisses me on the cheek. "And remember, *Father* Stephen, Proverbs says that there is wisdom in many counselors. So spill it. What happened today with you and Anthony?"

Chapter 11

I tell all the details to S & M and Father Grissom about what has been happening between Anthony and me. I start at the beginning.

"Once I moved into my apartment at Mockingbird Place we became close friends, but I wanted much more. I just couldn't tell him how I felt, knowing that he wasn't ready since he'd been through so much. Little by little he shared some about his past, but most I learned through Nicco. One day I thought the moment was right to kiss him, so I did. But I was wrong. Anthony left without saying a word and wouldn't talk to me for several days. When he did he was very cold. It went on like that for months."

"But something changed, right?"

"Yeah. After the fight with O'Brien, you remember Anthony let me take him to the hospital, and his walls seemed to come down some. The next day he came to my apartment, and I told him how I felt. He marched out the door. I wanted to go after him, but I didn't. I wasn't sure what else I could do or say that would change anything."

"I'm so sorry, Stephen," Martha says.

"The worst of it for me was when Anthony told me that he loved me."

From the look on their faces I can tell that fact clearly shocked them.

"What did you say?" Sarah leans forward. "Anthony told you he loved you?"

I sigh. "Yes, but it wasn't real. It was when I visited him at the hospital and the drugs were still in his system." Confessing to them is making my guilt resurface. "Even though I knew better, I let him kiss me. When I went back to see him and the drugs were almost gone, his walls were back up." I look at them. "I won't give up. I just can't. I love him too much. But I don't know what to do."

"I think we can help you." Martha stands. "But do you mind if we take this out to the pool first? I need a cigarette."

Sarah hops up from the sofa. "Me, too. Good idea, sweetheart."

Father Grissom smiles and pulls out a couple of cigars from his jacket. "I think we can join them, Stephen. I know you're not much of a smoker, but I remember you enjoyed a cigar with me during my last visit to Dallas."

"Sure," I answer, standing. "Maybe it will help to relax me."

Martha smiles. "Since it's such a beautiful day, why don't we take our wine outside?"

Sarah lifts the empty bottle. "I'll grab a fresh one for us."

When we get outside, Father Grissom and I grab a couple of the pool chairs and place them next to the bench under Malcolm's memorial tree. I glance at the stone marker and plaque that remind me of the great man who once lived here. It wasn't that long ago that we had the dedication service for it, the same day that Nicco got out of prison. The granite vase that S & M had installed next to the marker a couple of months back is filled with beautiful fresh flowers. Every resident of Mockingbird Place takes turns making sure the vase is never empty. My turn is next week. I plan on putting in sunflowers, since I know they're Martha's favorite flower. Sarah's is roses, so that will be the next kind I get.

Martha and Sarah settle down on the bench and light their cigarettes. Father Grissom hands me a cigar and we both take a puff. I let the warm smoke roll around in my mouth and then blow it out slowly. I feel the muscles in my shoulders untighten just a bit.

Sarah looks at the flowers in the vase. "I'm sure if Malcolm were here, he would say the perfect thing to help you, Stephen. God, he was such a wonderful man. M and I wouldn't be together if it weren't for Malcolm." She puts her arm around Martha. "Stephen, I had walls of my own a long time ago. Back then I was in the closet."

"Everyone was, sweetheart," Martha says. "Society wasn't like it is today."

"That's the truth." Father Grissom holds his cigar like a pointer. "People call them the good old days, but it was much harder for many. Today may not be perfect, but it is better in a lot of ways."

"I agree," Sarah says. "I was filled with shame for being a lesbian, for being the real me, and I pulled away from Martha. Malcolm saw right through me. He asked me if I'd ever told Martha how I felt. And went on to say that I might be surprised to know she felt the same way. Well, as you can see now I did finally tell her." Sarah kissed her lightly on the cheek. "And we've been together ever since."

"I'm so glad," I say. "You two are the perfect couple."

"Have you ever told Anthony about your past?" she asks.

I shake my head. "No. Like I said a little bit ago, it's not something I talk about much."

Martha looks at me. "Why not?"

"I don't know. They are just memories I don't like to bring up or burden other people with. It's best left in the past. I'm a very different person than I was then."

She nods. "And so is Anthony, but both of you are who you are today because of the pain you went through. Like it or not, the past is still part of you. It's not something to be ashamed of or hidden away."

"They are completely right," Father Grissom says. "Do you think less of Anthony because of what he went through?"

"Of course not. I think he's amazing and strong."

"And guess what? He won't think less of you either."

"Amen, Father," Martha says. "In fact, I'm pretty sure he will see the same things in you even more once you tell him everything. You're amazing and strong and wonderful."

Sarah nods in agreement. "The reason I've told you my story, Stephen, is you need to be honest with Anthony about your past."

Father Grissom takes another puff on his cigar. "I believe since you had the courage to share your past with us, you're the one who should open up to him first."

Their words give me hope. Maybe there is a way to reach Anthony. I never thought telling him about my past would help us to be together.

"I know his walls are up again, but once I'm able to see Anthony, I *will* tell him."

AS THE SUN dips down below the horizon, I look at my trio of advisors. They have given me so much hope that Anthony and I still have a chance to be together.

Sarah pours the last few drops of the second bottle of wine into her glass. "Well, that's the last of it."

Father Grissom stands. "I need to get back to my hotel. I have an early flight in the morning."

"And S and I have some cleaning to do." Martha puts out her cigarette and gets up from the bench.

"I'd love to help," I say.

"Not a chance." Sarah winks. "I believe you've got some serious thinking to do tonight, Stephen."

"I sure do. Thank you all so much." I give each of them a hug. "Say a prayer for Anthony and me."

"We will," Father Grissom says. "Right, ladies?"

"Right," they answer him in unison.

I walk back into my apartment. I'm so glad I talked with them. They gave me such hope that Anthony and I still have a chance.

Now I just have to figure out when to tell him about my past. Talking to him at the hospital about it is out of the question. What about when he comes home tomorrow? Is that too soon? Probably. I should give him more time to fully recover, but I'm just so anxious.

Sarah was right. I do have some serious thinking to do tonight. I head upstairs to take a nice, warm shower. That's when and where I always do my best thinking.

The warm water and the two glasses of wine I enjoyed at the pool work together to really relax me. Even though I should be planning how to tell Anthony about my past, all I can think about is how much I want to spend the rest of my life with him. He's the future I hope for.

So much for serious thinking time.

As I step out of the shower and dry off, my mind keeps replaying the moment he told me he loved me. I lick my lips, remembering his kiss that was even better than I could have imagined.

I get into my bed.

As I begin to drift off, I whisper, "I love you, Anthony."

Chapter 12

I stop and look up at the mountain I'm trying to climb. It's so high and treacherous that I can't see the top of it from here. "Will I ever make it?"

"You must," a warm voice answers to my left.

I glance in the direction it came from, and see a castle with thick walls of stone. "Who said that?"

"It's me, Stephen."

"Anthony?"

"Please, don't give up. Keep climbing."

I look back at the rising cliffs before me. "But it's so high. I don't know if I can do it."

When I turn back to the castle, it's gone. Instead I see Anthony in the hospital bed.

"I love you." His words echo in my ears.

Without warning, the impenetrable castle is back. I know he's inside and I can't get to him. The only thing I know to do is to climb the mountain. That will at least allow me to see over the castle's walls.

Using my hands, I find indentions in the rock and pull myself up. It's slow going at first, but I find a rhythm that increases my pace. When I take a second to catch my breath, I look back down and realize I'm halfway up the mountain. From this vantage, I see Anthony whispering to O'Brien. I can't quite make out *the words where I am holding on, but I don't have to. I've memorized them and they still crush me, knowing why Anthony says them. "You'll never hurt me again, you fucking pedophile."*

I squint, trying to focus my sight on Anthony.

The fighting cage morphs back into the castle, and to my surprise the walls are crumbling.

"I love you. Don't give up." Anthony's words are faint, rising up from below me.

"I love you, too. I won't give up. I promise."

Is it my climbing that's causing his walls to crumble? I'm not sure, but if it is, I have to get to the top. I have to free Anthony from that prison. He needs me, and I need him.

Though I'm exhausted, I double my climbing efforts. It seems like hours to gain a few feet. Eventually, I see the snow-capped top of the peak and my heart soars. I look down again, but I'm too far up to see the castle any longer. Still, in my heart, I have to believe its walls are almost gone.

The last inches of my climb are the hardest. I'm holding on with both hands, feet dangling. Below me is a terrifying drop. But if I can just reach that next indention in the rock, I can make it to the top. Anthony will be free of those damn walls.

"Come on, Stephen," his voice encourages me. "You can do it. You must do it. Come on."

The wind at this elevation is icy and cuts through me like a knife. My muscles are drained. My energy is spent. There's nothing left in the tank.

I can feel my grip loosening. I know that if I let go I'm dead, but I can't hold on much longer. This is it. It's over. "I love you, Anthony. I'm sorry I failed you."

My fingers slip and I start to drop. But then, from above, a hand grabs hold of my arm, lifting me to the top of the mountain.

When I land on my feet, I ignore the incredible view around me but instead stare into the most gorgeous brown eyes I've ever seen. Anthony is wearing his boxing shorts.

"It's you," I say to him. "But how?"

"You did it, sweetheart." He smiles, sending a warm shock that zips through my body. "You never stopped trying. Those walls are gone between us. Forever."

"Forever? Really?"

He smiles and nods. Then he kisses me and the whole world seems to vibrate around us.

I wrap my arms around him and we fall to the mat in the cage. For a fleeting moment, I wonder why there's a fighting cage on the top of this mountain. But when Anthony squeezes my cock through my jeans, my mind lets that moment go, fixing on a potent, urgent desire.

"And I want you, my love." He rips off my shirt. "I want all of you."

"I want you, too. I want you now." I slip his T-shirt over his head and toss it into the air.

Filled with awe and gratitude for this perfect moment, I watch as his shirt sails down the mountain. Then I let my eyes delight in his muscled chest. "You're flawless, Anthony."

His laugh echoes off the sides of the cliffs. "Hardly flawless, sweetheart," he says, and then slides his sinful tongue over my nipples, one at a time.

To my absolute thrill, he strips out of the rest of his clothes. His big, thick cock is stiff.

"I've waited a long time for this," I confess, slipping out of my jeans and underwear.

He gives me a wicked wink. "Far too long, but I'm fixing that."

"Yes, you are," I say in my most seductive tone.

He flips around on his side, leaving us in the perfect spot to suck on each other's cock—a yummy sixty-nine.

Unable to resist, I run my tongue up and down his shaft. I can feel him doing the same to me. There's a fire inside me—an unquenchable and lusty blaze. I lap up the salty, slick drop that sits on the tip of his dick. It's a little pearl that gives a promise of more. And I want more. So much more.

I swallow him and feel him swallow me. Every part of me burns with hunger for him. We're connected on a primal level, and it's driving me to the very edge of all that is sane. But I don't want to be sane. Not here. Not with him. I want to surrender to every wild passion, every crazy pleasure, every delirious sensation that he offers me.

He flips back around, diving between my legs. As he sucks on my cock, I lean back on my elbows, relishing the feel of his mouth on me.

"That feels so good," I tell him.

"And you taste good. So good," he whispers lustily before swallowing me whole once again.

"Oh, yes! That's it. Just right. Mmm. So close, Anthony."

He cups my balls and squeezes them just enough to drive me wild. "Come for me, baby. Let go. I want to drink up your pleasure. Give me every drop, sweetheart." His sucking intensifies, and it pushes me to the edge.

"Ahhh." As my entire body convulses in an explosion of release, I shoot into his thirsty mouth.

He slides up next to me and wraps me in his arms. "I love you."

"I love you, too. I've been waiting for this for so long."

He smiles. "I'm the one who's been waiting the longest, Stephen, if you'll remember."

"No, Anthony. I've wanted you since the first time I laid eyes on you," I tease back. "It's me, not you, who has been patient."

He shakes his head and grins. "Nope. When I saw you the first time, I wanted to drag you then and there to my bed. Beat that, Mister."

"I'll beat something," I laugh, and then grab his cock. "But I'm the one who waited. And waited. And waited."

"So? You want more of me?" He laughs. "You think you can take me?"

"I sure do. I don't play fair, Anthony. Admit that I'm the one who waited the longest and you'll be very happy." I stroke his cock and then let go. "What do you say?"

"I'll say anything but just don't let go again. You win, Stephen. You waited the longest."

We both laugh until we are in hysterics.

I LAUGH until tears fall down my cheeks. I open my eyes, and realize it was just another dream. "Damn. Why do I always have to wake up so soon?"

Chapter 13

s the dream of Anthony fades away, I reach for my phone on the nightstand. Nicco's name is on the caller ID.

"Hello, Nicco."

"Hey, Stephen. Just wanted to let you know that Anthony and I just got back home."

"What time is it?"

"Ten."

"Really?"

"Yes. I didn't wake you, did I?"

"You did, but that's okay." I jump out of the bed. "Today is my day off, but I shouldn't have slept in so long. How's Anthony doing?"

"He's fine. I know it's your day off, but do you mind coming over? I want to stock the fridge and pantry, plus I need to run by the pharmacy to fill his prescription."

"I don't mind, but what if he doesn't want me there?"

"You and I both know what happened at the hospital. You two need to talk."

"Yes, we do. But shouldn't I wait until he's back on his feet?"

Nicco laughs. "He's fine, Stephen. Just come on over. I'll put on a pot of coffee for the both of you."

"Okay. Give me ten minutes." I put the phone away and dress.

I hope this is the right time for me to talk with Anthony like Nicco believes. I'm ready to tell Anthony about my past, even though I'm also a little nervous. *Please God, help me.*

I RING the doorbell of Unit J. The door opens, and I'm surprised to see Anthony instead of Nicco.

"Come on in," Anthony says. "The coffee is ready."

"Where's your brother?"

"I'm here, Stephen," Nicco calls from the kitchen. "Just getting my keys. I really appreciate this."

"I can take care of myself, bro. I'm feeling so much better. I don't need a sitter."

"Not your call right now. Besides, I don't want to worry about you. Stephen, I'll call you when I'm headed back."

"I'll be here," I say. "I'm glad to know that Anthony's condition has greatly improved since I last saw him."

"Improved? I'm just fine. Really."

I smile. "I know you are, but I want to talk to you."

Anthony looks at me with those piercing eyes of his. "Okay."

"Bye, guys." Nicco walks out the back door, leaving Anthony and me alone.

"I could use a cup of coffee," Anthony says, leading me into the kitchen. "I made Nicco stop and get donuts after we left the hospital. Would you like some?"

"Sounds great." I remember the last time he and I shared donuts. Harvey's donuts. I sure hope this time ends better than that day.

We sit down at the table.

"So, Stephen. What do you need to talk about?" His tone is cold and distant.

Maybe he still doesn't feel good and is just putting on an act. Is he in any condition to listen to what I have to tell him? It can wait.

But Nicco told me that Anthony was fine. If Anthony is putting on an act, it's to push me away again. But guess what? He's not going to get away with it.

Okay, Stephen. Just let it out.

"I've been meaning to share this with you for some time but never found the right opportunity." I take a deep breath and begin telling him about my childhood.

His harsh demeanor softens with every detail I share. The last thing I tell him is about the crash that killed Father O'Malley and his wife, Ellen. When I finish, he looks down into his cup. We sit there in painful silence for several heart-wrenching moments.

Was I wrong to tell him today? He did just get out of the hospital. Oh, God. Did I blow it?

There are tears in his eyes. "Stephen, I had no idea."

I'm surprised when he reaches across the table and grabs my hand. When he squeezes it, I feel like maybe he's ready to open up. He stands and moves next to me. So close. Are his walls down?

He lightly presses his mouth to mine and pulls me to my feet. I melt into him, loving the taste of his lips.

"I'm so sorry, Stephen," he says with his lips still touching my mouth.

Before I can respond, he deepens his kiss and wraps his arms around me. I put my arms around him as he pulls me in closer. This is what I've dreamed of, being together, holding each other.

He starts to unbutton my shirt, causing heat to roll through me. Heat for him. Heat that has been inside me since the first day I met him. Is this real or am I still dreaming?

"Let's take this to my bedroom." His tone is deep, primal, and oh so sexy. "I want you."

My heart is pounding in my chest. He wants me. I want him. But then a bit of concern bubbles up to the surface inside me. "Anthony, this is too fast."

He brushes his lips to my neck, causing a shiver through my

body that reaches down between my legs. My defenses are weak. I want him.

His touches are heating me up. We continue kissing until I can feel my lips throbbing and my cock getting hard. I want this. But I can't. "No, Anthony. Not yet. Not now."

He whispers seductively in my ear. "Stephen, you need this as much as I do. Let's stop playing games and enjoy each other's body. We've waited far too long."

His words are mesmerizing. He's right. I do need him, and I'm ready to stop playing games. It has been far too long. "I love you, Anthony. I love you so much."

He keeps kissing and touching me. "Let's stop putting it off and go to my bedroom."

As much as I want him, this doesn't feel right. "Wait. Stop."

He leans back slightly, keeping his hands on my body. "What? What's the matter?"

"I'm not sure." I look in his eyes, his sexy alluring eyes. "Why?"

"Why what?"

"Why do you want to take me to your bedroom?"

He grins wickedly. "Haven't I made that clear? For sex, of course. Don't you want to?"

"Yes. More than anything."

"Then what the hell is wrong with you?" His tone is full of frustration.

I can feel his walls are up. Maybe they were never down. Is this sudden push for sex his way of not opening up to me? "Anthony, I have to know that there's more to this than just sex."

"Why are you doing this?" He steps back, obviously aggravated with me. "We're two gay men who turn each other on. We deserve this pleasure, don't we?"

"There's more to this than just pleasure. I love you. I want this to be forever. And you've only told me you loved me when you were still on those drugs. Was that the truth or just the drugs? Do you love me? Do you want to be with me, not just for a hookup but forever?"

"Forever? Who does forever? You should know better. There is no forever."

"I don't believe that. Look around us, Anthony. There are examples of people that prove forever does exist. S & M lived in a time when it was a crime to be gay, but they overcame the odds. Oliver and Adam on paper shouldn't have worked out, but they did. Neither should have Trace and Luke or Eli and Jackson, not to even mention Maddox and Jaris. Besides, you're just making excuses, using sex to avoid what's really going on inside you." I can see a storm of emotions in his eyes. As difficult as this is, I have to push him to admit the truth. It's the only way. "You love me. I know it. You know it. Why won't you admit it?"

"Because I don't believe in anything. Not forever. Not God. Not hope. And especially not love."

His words are like daggers to my soul. *Please God. Please. Help me help him.*

"All I can give you is sex," he says. "Friends with benefits. Obviously, that's not enough for you, but I don't have any more inside me. You should give up. I'm a lost cause."

"I will never give up on you or us. You are not a lost cause. No one is."

"Damn it, don't be naïve. You thought forever was going to happen with that priest and his wife, but they were killed. You were left alone."

His words cut me to the core. "Why are you doing this? Using my own life against me? You don't have to answer. I already know. You're afraid to let your guard down, to show me your true feelings. So you're doing all in your power to make me give up and surrender. Listen to me, mister, and listen good. I'm not going anywhere. I love you. I will always love you. That's not going to change. No matter how many times you break my heart with your hurtful words, I will never give up."

Anthony's lips move as if he's trying to think of something to say to me. But nothing comes out. He closes his eyes and takes a deep breath.

My phone rings, breaking the spell. Anthony opens his eyes, looks at me, and then goes up the stairs to his bedroom.

Did I do the right thing? Maybe I should have gone to his bed when he offered and worried about matters of the heart later. But that's not who I am.

I answer my phone.

Nicco asks. "How are you guys doing?"

"Not good. He's in his room."

"Damn."

"Yes. Damn. That's the correct word for it."

"Are you going to be able to work things out or should I come home?"

"Not today. That's for sure." I sigh, feeling my hope slipping away. "Come on home."

Chapter 14

I walk to the back of the church to shake hands with our members and visitors. It was tough to plow through this past week. Anthony hasn't said a single word to me since Monday when he came home from the hospital. His icy demeanor is killing me.

One of the parishioners shakes my hand. "Wonderful sermon, Father."

Even though I find that hard to believe since I've been so distracted of late, I say, "Thank you."

"We are all so glad you're here," his wife says. "You've reenergized this parish."

"Thank you, but it takes all of us."

She smiles. "I know. Like you said this morning, 'where two or three are gathered together...' See you next Sunday."

I'm shocked that so many seem to have been moved by my sermon. The truth is I was only going through the motions. It must have been God's doing, not mine.

Mrs. Clark steps up next. "How are you?"

"I'm fine."

"Really?" She grins. "Lying is a sin, Father Stephen. You

seemed like you had something on your mind during the service. Or someone? Perhaps someone special?"

I smile. "Some believe that reading another person's mind is also a sin, Mrs. Clark."

The dear woman places her hands on her hips in a clear act of defiance. "What about you? How do you feel about that?"

"I trust you always use your powers for good. But you're right. There is something on my mind and I would really appreciate your prayers."

"I always pray for you, Father. But I will double up on my efforts."

The last in the line to shake my hand are Harvey and Nathan.

"Do you know where S & M are?" I ask. "I didn't see them in their normal spot."

Harvey says, "Martha has been under the weather this week. Sarah probably stayed home with her. Jaris and Maddox checked in on Martha yesterday. They told Sarah that if Martha wasn't feeling better by Monday to take her to their office."

"I hope it isn't anything serious."

Nathan places his hand on my shoulder. "I'm sure she'll be fine. She's a very strong woman."

"That she is, but it doesn't hurt to have two great doctors that do house calls."

Harvey nods. "Or a wonderful, loving priest to say a prayer. Stephen, why don't you join Nathan and I for lunch? We found an incredible Mexican restaurant that just opened up on Cedar Springs. Their margaritas are fantastic."

"I can't turn down an invitation like that. I'd love to join you. Give me a few minutes to get out of these vestments and I'll meet you in the parking lot."

Twenty minutes later, I pull into a parking space right next to Harvey's Rolls-Royce. I'm more familiar with Harvey in his work truck than the Rolls, which is a reminder how wealthy he really is. I remember when I first met him that I had no clue he was one of the richest men in Texas.

Once we're seated and have given the waiter our order, I look across the table at another very happy couple. "How do you do it?"

"Do what, Stephen?" Harvey has a puzzled look on his face. So does Nathan.

"Make it work between you two. Or maybe a better question is how did you learn to trust each other? To let your walls down and be real?"

"This is about Tony, isn't it?" Harvey asks. "We all know how he's been acting with you since leaving the hospital."

"Yes. It's about him. He's all I can think about, night and day. I feel like I'm in a fog and can't get out. S & M and Father Grissom told me to open up to Anthony and that he would likely open up to me. I did. I told him everything. But it only seemed to make him shut me out even more than ever. He told me he loved me when he was in the hospital, but I think that was likely just the effects of the drugs. Maybe he doesn't love me at all. Maybe I'm just fighting a battle that I can never win. Maybe I've been deluding myself all this—"

"Hold on, young man," Harvey says firmly. "There's no doubt in my mind how much Tony loves you. We've all seen it in his eyes whenever you walk into the room. I've known that kid since Malcolm rescued him and moved him in with S & M. I've never seen him so miserable before."

My heart tightens in my chest hearing that word. *Miserable.*

"Harvey!" Nathan turns to him with scolding eyes.

"No, Nathan," I say. "Harvey's right. I am making Anthony miserable. I need to back off."

Harvey leans across the table and grabs my hand. "Didn't I tell you to hold on, young man?"

Nathan frowns.

"You too, sweetheart. Just let me explain. You both need to understand why Tony is miserable. It's because he's in turmoil. He wants you, Stephen, but he's afraid. Old patterns are hard to break. I know. When I was yours and Tony's age I was tied up like a knot. S & M's and Father Grissom's advice to you was right. You were honest with him. You were fearless and exposed everything about yourself to him. Like it says in the Bible, you've planted a seed. Now you have to water it, weed it, and let it grow."

I grin. "No fair using the Bible against me."

He chuckles. "All is fair in love, Father. I have no doubt that Tony will come around. You've just got to believe and be patient."

"Patience? That's the hard part, isn't it?"

They both nod.

The waiter brings us our margaritas.

Harvey shares with me how he'd once been in love with Malcolm but never acted on it because he was too afraid. The story is so heartbreaking. "The reason I told you this is to let you know that you have to just keep on keeping on, if you know what I mean."

"I think I do."

They continue to give me wonderful advice about how to deal with Anthony, as we enjoy the best Mexican food I've ever tasted. And Harvey was right. The margaritas are fantastic.

TOO MANY MARGARITAS LATER, I see Nicco, Eli, and Jackson walk into the restaurant. Harvey called them to come to our rescue because we aren't in any condition to drive.

"Hey, fellas," Eli, our resident fireman at Mockingbird Place, says with a grin. "How are you feeling?"

"We're feeling just fine. That's the problem." Harvey chuckles.

Nicco teasingly shakes his finger at the three of us. "Drunk on a Sunday afternoon. You should be ashamed of yourselves."

"Not drunk," I say with a grin. "Just happy."

"Happy and buzzing," Eli adds.

Nathan nods. "That's the gospel truth."

"Thanks for coming." Harvey reaches in his pocket. "Jackson, here are my keys to the Rolls."

"You've got to be kidding me. You want me to drive a car worth hundreds of thousands of dollars, Harvey?"

He grins. "It's insured, and it's just a car."

"It's not just a car to me." Jackson takes a deep breath.

Nicco nods. "More like a king's throne on wheels."

Nathan giggles. "Or queen's."

"Nathan! That's not nice." He busts out in hysterics.

We all laugh.

Once we gain our composure, Jackson says, "I guess there's no getting out of it. We can't leave Harvey's Rolls here overnight." He turns to me. "Father Stephen, would you mind saying a prayer for me?"

I laugh again, still feeling the effects of my three margaritas. "I will, but I'm sure you'll be fine."

"I hope you're right." He looks at Eli. "Honey, just know when you're following, I'm going to drive really slow, okay."

Eli kisses him. "Okay."

I hug Harvey and Nathan. "Thank you. I really appreciate the meal, the advice, but most of all those great margaritas."

Harvey laughs once again, and we all join in. He looks at Nathan. "Let's go, sweetheart. I feel nap eyes coming on."

"So do I, honey. So do I."

Nicco and I watch them walk out of the restaurant.

He holds out his hand. "I'm your driver, Stephen."

"Yes, you are." I give him my keys.

We walk to my car.

Nicco drives us out of the parking lot. "Stephen, there's something important I need to talk with you about. How buzzy are you?"

I can tell whatever is on his mind is very serious. "I really feel fine. I just knew I shouldn't drive. How about we stop for coffee and pie?"

"Won't that destroy your buzz?"

"It's already gone." I'm anxious to hear what he has to say. "Let's go to Lucy's."

"Sounds good to me."

The owner of the diner, whose name is actually Lucy, greets us. She's a throwback to the 50s and always wears her red hair the way her famous comedian namesake wore hers. "Father Stephen, have you come to eat dinner or do you want your usual, pie and coffee? And who is this good-looking man with you?"

"This is Nicco, Anthony's brother."

She shakes his hand. "It's very nice to meet you."

"Same here. I've heard so much about you, Lucy. Can't wait to try your food."

"You won't be disappointed," I say, turning back to Lucy. "We're here for my usual—pie and coffee."

"Excellent." She leads us to a booth. "I just put on a fresh pot. You two be thinking what kind of pie you want while I get your coffee."

She walks away.

"What kind of pie do you like, Nicco? Whatever it is I can guarantee it will be delicious."

"I love banana cream, if they have it."

"Oh, they have it all right, and it's delicious. I'm an apple man myself."

After we get our coffee and pies, I ask him, "So, did you want to talk to me about Anthony?"

"Yes."

"He's okay, isn't he?"

"He's good. In fact he's got a match on Wednesday."

"It's too soon for that, Nicco. He just got out of the hospital."

"I agree, but my brother is bullheaded. He told me that it was something he had to do. And you know him."

"Yes, I do. Maybe it will be good for him. He always seems so at peace after a fight."

"Except for the fight with O'Brien."

"That's true. I hope Anthony isn't trying to make a point. He always lets his opponent wail on him in the beginning of every fight."

Nicco nods. "I've noticed that. Do you know why he does that? Because I sure don't."

"He lets his opponents beat up on him so that he can get really angry. Then at a certain point he whispers something to them and starts hitting back much harder than they ever hit him."

"It's still strange. What does he whisper to them and why does he need to get angry? I still don't get it. Why take all those punches?

He's a great fighter. He could leave the cage unscathed almost every time."

"I believe it helps him to release all the pain and rage that is buried deep inside him."

"You really do know him better than anyone else. Has he opened up to you a little?"

"No. He hasn't even let me peek over his walls. O'Brien told me what he whispered in his ear just before Anthony gave him that concussion."

"What did he whisper to O'Brien?"

"He said, 'You'll never hurt me again, you fucking pedophile.'"

"Damn, why did that have to happen to my brother?"

"I don't know why he had to go through such a horrible experience. What I do know is that we've got to help Anthony put the past behind him."

"You're right. He's been a prisoner of those nightmares for far too long. Which brings me to what I need to talk with you about." Nicco takes a sip of his coffee, clearly to give him a moment to gather his thoughts. Whatever he has to say to me must be difficult for him. "I've been in touch with our mother."

My gut tightens. I've never met the woman, but I'm very angry with her. "You have?" I ask, trying to keep my tone level. "How was she?"

How could a mother let something like that happen to her own child? Anthony deserved better.

"She's been clean for a year now and goes to her meetings like clockwork. The first time I saw her I was shocked. She was dressed in a beautiful outfit and looked great. So opposite of how I remember her back when Anthony and I were living with her—drugged up and usually passed out."

I can see the hope and relief on Nicco's face, but I know that a high percentage of recovering addicts relapse. "And how do you feel about reconnecting with her?"

"At first I was so angry, but since we've seen each other several times I've been able to let it go. She's changed, Stephen. She's really changed. She's like the mother I remember before our dad died. I never thought I would ever be able to forgive her, but somehow I have." He points up. "Maybe God had something to do with that."

"Maybe so." I don't have any other explanation. Nicco spent years in prison for something he didn't do because of that woman. And Anthony suffered so much more. In fact, he's still suffering because of her.

"She feels terrible about what happened, that she let the drugs take over her life and caused her sons so much pain, especially Anthony."

"She should," I say, hearing the harshness in my voice.

He stops and looks at me in the eyes. "My mom was broken after Dad died, but I remember the way she was before. We had a clean house, food on the table, and she tucked us in every night and gave us a kiss. She was a true mother back then. It wasn't easy, but I did forgive her, because I do remember. But I don't know if my brother remembers. Anthony was so little when we lost Dad."

"Does Anthony know you've been talking with your mother?"

He shakes his head. "No. I wasn't sure I should tell him. He's got so much else to deal with. I'm worried that might push him over the edge, but then again it may be the key for his healing. I just don't know. She wants to see him. What should I do?"

"You know my answer to every problem or challenge you face."

He grins. "Pray first, right?"

"That's right."

"I have prayed, but I still don't know what to do."

"Then you don't do anything until you know for sure."

"Will you come with me to meet her? Then you can tell me what you think."

Yeah, I'll meet her, and I'll tell her exactly what I think of her. Oh God, you've got to help me with this.

Nicco needs my help, and I need to go for Anthony.

I take a deep breath. "Sure. I'll go with you to meet her."

Chapter 15

I 've been sitting under Malcolm's memorial tree hoping to figure out what I can say to Anthony and Nicco's mother. It's only two hours before I go with Nicco to meet her and I still have no clue.

I glance at the stone and plaque that honor Malcolm. "You have any ideas for me? I could sure use some."

I think about how that wonderful man helped so many, including Anthony. Malcolm took him out of the system after his mother lost custody and brought him to this place, where wounded souls find a family and a home. More than his own mother, Malcolm and S & M were parents to him. What a wicked woman. How could anyone forgive her? But Nicco has. Maybe I need a lesson from him, because right now I don't have it in me to forgive her.

"God, I'm not sure what to do. Was it a mistake to agree to meet her? I'm afraid that when I see her I'll tell her what I really feel." I close my eyes. "Please help me. I'm just so angry."

I feel the tears of rage dripping down my cheeks. I haven't been this angry in a very long time. My mind drifts back to when I was living at the orphanage.

. . .

FATHER O'MALLEY SENDS me into the basketball game, replacing Tommy. We're playing Marsh Lakes Junior High.

The score is tied 56-56.

I hear the boy closest to me from the other team whisper, "Bunch of orphan bastards. We can't let them beat us. Come on, guys."

I know there's only two minutes left to play, but we've scored the last four baskets. Our chances to win are really good.

I make a layup, putting us in the lead.

The score is 58-56.

My fellow orphan bastard teammates slap me on the back.

God, this is so much fun. I can't believe it took me so long to agree to play on Father O'Malley's team.

Gary, who we all call "Slim," fouls one of the other boys, giving him two chances at the free-throw line. The kid makes both, once again tying up the score at 58-58.

We get the ball, but when Kyle shoots and misses, the other team gets the rebound.

The clock is ticking. Only 10 seconds left.

Joey gets the ball away from the other team and passes it to Kyle, who trips. The ball goes rolling across the gym floor in the direction of Father O'Malley and Mr. Kimbell, the director of the orphanage. I chase after the ball.

I hear the crowd counting down—six…five…four…

I grab the ball before it goes out of bounds.

…three…two…

I throw as hard as I can at our basket, which looks like it's miles away. As the end-of-the-game horn sounds, the ball swooshes round and round the rim but miraculously falls through the net, winning us the game.

The final score is 60-58.

The crowd goes wild, and I'm surrounded by my teammates. I see Father O'Malley smiling and giving me the "thumbs-up" signal. He is so great and so is his wife. They have promised to take me out on my birthday next month. I can't wait.

The celebration from my buddies continues as we walk into the locker room.

Joey gives me a high-five. "We crushed those assholes, didn't we, Stephen?"

"We sure did." I just have to let Father O'Malley know how much I appreciate what he's done for me.

"Where you going, Stephen?" Kyle asks.

"I'll be back. Just need to find Father O'Malley."

As I walk down the hallway, I hear voices coming from Mr. Kimbell's office.

"You sure about that, Father?" Mr. Kimbell asks.

"I am. Keep Anthony here Friday. I don't want him going bowling with the other boys."

Angry tears well up in my eyes, and I turn around, running out the exit door. I'm so mad and hurt. How could he do this to me?

Passing the baseball field, I see his Ford Explorer parked in front of the building. I stop, remembering all the times I've rode in it with him. "Damn it. I should have never joined your stupid team. You're a liar, just like everyone else. Fucking bastard!"

As rage and disappointment boil inside me, I grab a bat that didn't make it back to the equipment room. He will pay for making me believe in fairy tales.

I run to his car and bash all the windows in with the bat. It doesn't make me feel any better, so I start hitting the hood, the doors, the lights, and every inch of it. But my anger and despair just keep on building.

"Anthony!" Father O'Malley yells.

I turn and see him running my direction. I have to get away. Away from him. He's a liar.

I run as fast as I can, but he catches me. I hit him as hard as I can. "Why? Why would you keep me from the bowling trip? I hate you! I hate you! Let me go!"

He doesn't release me but holds on tight.

"Please. Please let me go. You lied to me. You made me think I mattered to you, but I don't. You're just like everyone else. Please. Let me go." I lean my head into his chest and cry harder than I've ever cried before.

"Anthony, I didn't want you to go on the bowling trip because Ellen and I wanted to take you to Six Flags."

"What? But… Six Flags?" I wipe my eyes. "I've blown it again. Just like I always do. I'm a loser. I'll always be a loser. I'm sorry I busted up your car. You'll never forgive me."

He smiles. "I've already forgiven you, Anthony."

"You have? But look at your car."

"Oh, you'll be helping me pay for the repairs. My lawn needs mowing and I think Ellen wants to paint the living room. But I have forgiven you."

"HE FORGAVE me after all I did."

Where did this help come from? Malcolm? Father O'Malley? God? *Maybe all three.*

I look up into the sky as the breeze blows through Malcolm's tree. "Thank you."

I leave the bench and walk to my apartment to get ready to meet Anthony's mom.

NICCO PULLS his car in front of his mother's rental house, which is located about an hour from Dallas in Weatherford. It looks like someone has been taking good care of it. The lawn is mowed. The bushes are trimmed. There are even colorful flowers near the front steps. Is his mother the one responsible or the landlord? I wonder.

As we walk up to the front door, I feel anxious. My hands are clammy. I want to get this right. *Especially for Anthony.*

Nicco knocks on the door and it opens.

The woman who gave birth to him and Anthony stands in front of us, looking even more anxious than I feel. I thought she would be disheveled—hair messed up, wrinkled clothes, too much makeup. But instead I see a very attractive woman who is completely put together. Her long, raven hair complements her enchanting brown eyes. She wears a white top and black slacks.

She kisses Nicco on the cheek and then looks at me. "Hello, Father. Thank you so much for coming."

"Hello, Mrs. Mantonvani."

"Please come in and have a seat." Despite her outward calm, her hands shake ever so slightly.

We walk inside her home, which is lovely and just as well maintained as the outside.

I sit on the sofa next to Nicco.

"Would you like something to drink?" she asks. "I have coffee and tea, or water if you'd prefer."

I'm pretty sure that getting drinks for us would help calm her nerves. "Coffee, please. I take it black."

"Niccolo?"

"Coffee is great, Mom."

"I'll be right back. Please make yourselves at home." She walks into the kitchen.

I spot some photos on top of a piano, and realize they are of Nicco and Anthony when they were children. To get a better look, I stand and walk over to the piano.

Nicco comes up beside me.

I pick up the middle one with the young couple and their two children. "How old are you in this picture?"

"I think I was six or seven. Anthony was one or two." Nicco sighs. "That's the last Mantonvani family photo we ever took."

"You and Anthony look a lot like your dad."

"Yes, they do," his mother says, returning from the kitchen with a tray that has our coffees and some cookies. "I hope you like chocolate chip, Father. I made them myself this morning."

"Thank you. That's very nice of you."

A little smile appears on her face, which reminds me of Anthony a bit.

After we all sit down, she in the chair across from Nicco and me on the sofa, there's an awkward silence. It's evident that none of us are certain how to start the conversation.

Finally, she breaks the silence. "Father, Niccolo told me how you helped get his name cleared so that he was released from prison." Her eyes fill with tears. "I can't thank you enough. I was so filled with drugs that I failed him. I'm responsible for the years he lost in prison. I don't know how he's been able to forgive me, but I'm so glad he has. I certainly don't deserve to be forgiven."

"None of us do, Mrs. Mantonvani."

"I guess that's true." She makes the sign of the cross. "Please, call me Carlotta, Father."

"Of course." I take a sip of my coffee. "We all have done things that we're ashamed of."

"But not like me. Not like what I've done, ruining my children's lives because of my addiction." She looks down at her hands and her tone gets quieter and quieter. "I don't remember much after I got hooked. It's all hazy. All I could think of was when and where I could get my next fix. And my poor boys suffered so much." She closes her eyes. "I'm so ashamed."

Nicco gets up and puts his arm around her. "That's the past, Mom."

"Yes, but you and Anthony are still dealing with the fallout I caused." She looks at me, tears rolling down her cheeks. "I was always crazy or passed out when that bastard was hurting Anthony. What kind of mother lets that happen?"

I wish I had an answer for her, but I don't. It's hard to think about the damage she did to Nicco and Anthony. Yet, how can I judge her? Though I've always dreamed of meeting my biological parents one day, I never knew them. Maybe that's a blessing. Who knows what kind of damage they might have done to me?

"You can't keep beating yourself up, Mom," Nicco says. "Maybe you should tell Stephen how you got started on drugs. Give him the full picture."

She shakes her head. "That doesn't matter. I'm to blame. For everything."

Maybe that's true, but it's hard not to see the guilt she's carrying. "Please, Carlotta. Tell me. I want to know. Why don't you start at the beginning? The way I see you now and what I've heard from Nicco, it must have been desperation for you to have taken the first drug."

"In a way, yes. I asked a neighbor to watch my two boys so I could go to a bar to have just one drink. My husband had been dead for three months and I was barely holding it together. I thought I needed a break. You see, my husband, Francesco was my prince. He rescued me from my past and from myself. I was already on a road of self-destruction when he found me. Father, I've never told anyone about my childhood until I was in rehab. Niccolo doesn't even know the whole story."

He looks surprised. "I don't?"

"No, son. You don't."

"Please, Carlotta, tell us," I say. "Don't you think it's time to share this with your son?"

"Yes, Father. I do. My parents were alcoholics. They lived to drink. The fruit doesn't fall far from the tree, does it? I went days without food or seeing them when I was very young. I learned to steal from the local store to survive. I got caught one day. From then on, my parents locked me in the closet every time they left. One time I was trapped for four days without any food or water."

"My God, Mom."

Imagining Carlotta as a child treated so horribly helps me to understand her and how she checked out totally when her husband died.

She looks at me. "But I know none of that is any excuse for what I did to my boys. Believe me. I'm the guilty one. Instead of finding solace from a bottle or needle, I should have gone to a counselor. I know that now. That one drink I went to the bar for didn't suffice. So I had another. And another. And another. I ended up getting smashed. A guy, I don't even remember his name, took me to his place. He was an addict and introduced me to crystal meth. The first time I snorted the powder, a kind of euphoria came over me that took away my pain. That very night I was hooked. Nothing else mattered to me but getting high from then on." She covers her face with her hands and starts to sob. "I'm the one to blame for everything."

It's obvious to me that reaching down into those old memories has drained her.

"It's okay, Mom." Nicco hugs her. "I finally understand why you did what you did. It's a miracle you even survived."

She wipes her eyes, gaining her composure. "It's a miracle that you and Anthony survived. And it's a miracle that you were able to forgive me." She turns to me. "Father, I need another miracle. I just want to see Anthony. I don't expect him to forgive me, but I need to tell him how sorry I am. Will you help me?"

"I really wish I could, but Anthony isn't talking to me." I see the hope in hers and Nicco's eyes start to dim. "I'm not sure how I will get him to agree to meet you, but I'll do my best. You realize there's no way to know how he will react when he sees you. Are you sure you want to do this, Carlotta?"

"I must try to do this. I owe him at least that much."

"Okay, then. I'll see what I can do."

Chapter 16

My doorbell rings at 6:45pm. I know there's not a chance that it's Anthony, though with all my heart I wish it were. He's got his match tonight, so I'm sure he's already at the arena.

Anthony has made it very clear that he doesn't want to see or talk to me. I've tried to reach out to him, leaving him voicemails, knocking on his door, even putting a note on his car's windshield.

No response. Nothing. Nada.

There must be a way that I can reach him, but nothing I've done has worked. I'm hoping that Nicco's idea about tonight will finally give me a chance to talk to Anthony. I have so much to say to him. About his mother. About us. About everything.

I open my door and find Nicco standing on my steps.

"You ready to go?" he asks.

"Yeah, but honestly, I'm not sure how your brother is going to take an ambush after his fight. You sure we should do this?"

"Anthony has a thick skull. Sometimes you have to have a sneak attack and get in a hard punch to get his attention. What else do we have to lose?"

"I hope nothing."

"Me, too. I'll drive."

"Okay." I take a deep breath, step out of my apartment next to him, and lock my door. "Let's go."

We walk to his Honda Accord, which Harvey helped him get after he got out of prison.

As he drives out of Mockingbird Place's parking lot, my mind starts running over and over what I should say to Anthony. I really hope that he won't shut me out and will listen. But who knows? I might just run straight into those damn walls of his again.

Wanting to think about something else on the drive to the arena, I say. "Jaris and Maddox told me you left their practice for a job at the airport."

"I did." He grins. "I bet you're wondering why."

"I am. So?"

"I wanted to get something on my own. Call it pride. I am grateful to Jaris and Maddox for hooking me up at their practice, but office work isn't my thing. I really wanted something different. I met this guy who operates a charter out of Love Field. It's still office work, but I get to be around planes. And he's going to teach me how to fly. He's got his instructor license. You may not know this about me, but I've always wanted to be a pilot."

"I didn't know that. Good for you. What kind of charters does your friend have?"

"Right now, he only has one plane. He mainly flies people to Vegas, but he's got big plans to expand. When I get my license he hopes to buy another plane and make me a partner."

"It's good to hear that your future looks bright. If anyone deserves a real break, it's you, buddy."

"Thanks, Stephen. I'm really excited about this prospect."

"Who is this guy?"

"Gage McBain."

"I met him about a year ago, at one of Harvey and Nathan's parties."

"That's funny. I met him at one of their parties a few weeks ago."

I wonder if Gage hit on Nicco, like he did me. "You know, the guy has quite the reputation as a player in gay circles. It's my understanding that he's left a long trail of broken hearts."

"Oh, really?" Nicco's face darkens. "I didn't know that. The guy hit on me."

Is Nicco gay? He's never told me he was, so I just assumed he was straight. Who knows? Maybe Anthony knows? Maybe not.

Nicco drives into the arena's parking lot, causing my mind to swirl once again. What can I say to Anthony that will turn him around and not push me further away? *Please, God. Please.*

NICCO and I take our seats next to the rest of our neighbors. We're all anxious about this fight, especially since Anthony has only been out of the hospital for what seems like a blink of an eye, though it's really been over a week.

I'm glad to see O'Brien and his fiancée sitting next to S & M's left. He looks fully recovered. She looks very happy. Actually, they both look absolutely joyous. Joe, O'Brien's trainer, walks up and takes a seat next to them.

The announcer grabs the microphone. "Ladies and gentlemen, this fight is three rounds in the middleweight division. Introducing first, fighting out of the blue corner, a freestyle fighter with a professional record of twelve wins and one loss. He stands six feet 2 inches tall, weighing in at one hundred eighty-five pounds, from Kansas City, Missouri, it's John 'The Basher' Jacobson."

A mix of boos and cheers erupt from the audience as Jacobson steps forward, slamming his gloves together.

"Seems like more boos than cheers to me," Nicco says with a proud brotherly smile.

"To me, too. Anthony is always the favorite when he fights here."

"And now, introducing his opponent, who is no stranger to this arena, fighting out of the red corner, a freestyle fighter with an undefeated professional record of nineteen wins and zero losses. He stands five feet ten inches tall, weighing in at one hundred seventy-nine pounds, a hometown boy from right here in Dallas, it's Tony 'The Beast' Mantonvani."

Once again the crowd cheers, but this time I can only hear a few boos. It's all cheers in our section, with S & M being the loudest.

Anthony swings his arms wide to his sides, which is something I've seen him do before.

"Damn it, my brother's crazy," Nicco says. "He's signaling to the other guy that he's not going to block his punches."

I sigh. "Sure seems that way to me."

"What the hell is he thinking? Will he ever learn?"

"I sure hope so."

"When the action begins, our referee in charge is Allan Blackstone," the announcer says.

A girl in a swimsuit walks up holding the placard indicating the first round of the match.

Anthony and his opponent charge out to the center of the cage, and to my utter surprise, Anthony wails into the guy, landing a series of powerful punches and kicks. Unlike all his previous fights I've seen, he's not holding back at all. The other guy doesn't have a chance.

Why the sudden change in fighting tactics from Anthony? Is it because of what happened to O'Brien? Is Anthony worried that if he lets his opponent punch him into that familiar state of rage, he might really hurt him?

Anthony grabs the dazed fighter, holding him tight in a bear hug. And like always, I see him whispering in his opponent's ear.

Thanks to O'Brien, I believe I know what he's saying. *"You'll never hurt me again, you fucking pedophile."* But could it be something else since he's not in a rage? Or is he in a rage?

One hard punch to the chin and Anthony's opponent falls to the mat for the count.

I jump to my feet, cheering as loud as I can, as the crowd roars. I look over and see O'Brien is also on his feet.

Though a little dazed, Jacobson gets up with the help of his trainer.

The announcer calls the fight. "Ladies and gentlemen, referee

Allan Blackstone has called a stop to this contest at two minutes fifteen seconds of the very first round, declaring the winner by knockout Tony 'The Beast' Mantonvani."

Once again, the entire place erupts, as Anthony leaves the cage with his trainer. I'm so glad the fight ended this way, especially knowing it could have been so much worse.

But now that the fight is over, I have to face my biggest challenge.

AS NICCO and I head to the locker room, we pass a reporter and camera crew talking to Jacobson. A few people are gathered around them.

"He's a helluva fighter, that's for sure," Jacobson admits.

Nicco and I stop a few steps away to listen in, curious to hear what he has to say.

"I saw Mantonvani whisper something to you just before that last punch," the reporter says. "What did he say?"

"It was so fucking weird. He called me a pedophile. I'm no goddamn pedophile."

"He did? What exactly did he say?"

"Mantonvani grabbed me and said, 'You'll never hurt me again, you fucking pedophile.'"

Nicco whispers to me, "Shit, that's going to be all over the news tomorrow."

"Probably." I'm actually shocked it hasn't come out before now.

Jacobson looks at the reporter. "Why in the hell do you think he would say that to me?"

"I have no idea," he says. "But I'm going to try to find out."

I don't tell them that I have a good idea why Anthony always says that in a match. He's not talking to his opponent. He's talking to his dead abuser. It's his way of coping with the pain.

"Let's go, Nicco."

He nods, and we continue down the hall to the locker room.

The door opens, and Anthony's trainer walks out. "Hey, Nicco. Father."

Nicco shakes his hand. "Another great fight, Sam."

Sam smiles. "Best one yet. That boy is a champ, no doubt about it." He points at the door. "He's in there. I'll be back. I need to talk to the promoter."

He leaves and we walk inside.

Wearing only his trunks, Anthony sits on a bench. He looks up at Nicco and then at me. "What the hell are you doing here?"

"We need to talk," I say.

"I don't think so."

Nicco steps forward. "Anthony, you need to listen to what Stephen has to say."

"No, I don't." Anthony stares at me. "We've already said all that needs to be said to one another. He wants something from me I'm not able to give."

"Hey, stop being an ass." I'm aggravated with him, and why not? He has been a stubborn asshole, especially to me. "Sure, I want to revisit that discussion because we haven't said all that needs to be said to each other. At least I haven't. But there's something else I need to talk to—"

The door swings open and the camera crew and reporter rush in.

I become one hundred percent protective because I know the reporter wants to ask Anthony about what he whispered to Jacobson.

"Hold on." I swing my arms as wide as I can, similar to how Anthony had done in the cage, trying to block the reporter and camera crew from moving forward to him. "Mr. Mantonvani isn't taking interviews right now. You need to step out."

"Stephen, I'll talk to them," Anthony says sharply. "Let them through."

"No. You're not talking to anyone." Nicco's tone leaves no room for argument. "At least not yet."

"Okay. You heard them, folks," Anthony says to the reporter and camera crew. "Give us ten minutes."

"We'll be right outside the door, Tony," the reporter says.

I keep my arms wide until they walk out of the locker room, then I turn to face Anthony.

"So why the delay, Nicco, and why, Stephen, did you go all testosterone on that reporter?"

I sigh. "Because Jacobson just told that reporter what you whispered in his ear."

His eyes widen and he looks down. His voice lowers, as if he's talking to himself and not us, "Oh, my God. What am I going to tell them?" He looks at us. "You two don't know this, but I always whisper to my opponents—"

"We know, bro, and we can guess why. It's okay."

"No, it isn't. This could impact my career in the worst way." I can hear the uneasiness in his tone. "Inside the cage, when I get to that state and am able to whisper those words is the only time I feel normal and in control. What am I going to do?"

"How about tell them the truth," I answer.

"No one would understand the truth."

"I understand it. So does Nicco."

"Bro, you don't have any choice. Jacobson has let the cat out of the bag. You've got to deal with this head on like Stephen says."

Anthony takes a deep breath. "But how do I do that?"

I hate seeing him struggle with this. I can't imagine how hard it will be for him to share his truth with the world. "Listen, Anthony. The press already knows about your activism. You donate money and time to organizations that are supporting victims of child abuse. When you tell them your story it will connect the dots, let them find out why you're so passionate about those charities."

"You really think so?"

"I do."

"Okay, then. I'll do it. Give me a second before you let them back in. Nicco, would you go find Sam? He should be here when I bare my soul on camera."

"Of course. I'll be right back." Nicco walks out, leaving me alone with Anthony.

I can tell his walls are crumbling. More than any punch he's taken in a fight, the questions he'll be answering will pummel him even harder.

He puts on a T-shirt. "So? What did you need to talk to me about?"

"Too much to say in a few minutes, but it is important."

"Now I'm curious. Okay. Let's have a drink at J.R.'s in an hour. I'm sure I'll need one after the interview. Or two. Or three."

I smile. "That sounds great." I'm glad that his tone is less harsh than it has been of late, though I know he's suggesting the bar instead of one of our apartments to keep the playing field level between us.

"Stephen, do you really think it's going to be okay?"

Looking at him now, I can imagine the boy he once was—before the horror began in his life. "Yes, I do."

Nicco and Sam walk back into the locker room.

Sam walks over to Anthony and puts his arm around him. "It's going to be okay, my boy. I told you that you wouldn't be able to keep your secret forever."

"Yes, you did. It's just I wish it wasn't today."

"If wishes were fishes we'd all swim in the sea."

Anthony grins. "You sound like Martha."

"Smart woman, that Martha. She landed Sarah." He turns to me. "Father, would you mind letting in the vultures? Might as well get this over with."

"Sure thing." I open the door and look at the reporter. "He's ready to talk to you."

Chapter 17

Nicco pulls up to the curb next to J.R.'s. "You sure you don't want me to stay?"

"I'm sure." I get out of his car and lean in through the window. "I think telling Anthony about your mother's request might be better coming from me first. If he doesn't react well, then you have a second chance to talk to him about it later. If you're with me, he'll feel like we're ganging up on him and then your chance is gone."

"You're probably right. Besides, you two have a lot more to talk about than just my mom."

"We do. Thanks for dropping me off."

"My pleasure. Good luck, Stephen. I'll say a prayer for you."

"I'll need it. See you later."

As he drives away, I walk into J.R.'s. Since it's the middle of the week, there aren't very many people inside.

Anthony isn't here yet. I stayed for the interview, which he knocked out of the park. He still had to shower and change clothes. Actually, I'm glad to have a little time to myself to work out what to say to Anthony about his mother's request. I won't have too much time since he won't be long.

I grab two empty stools at the end of the bar. That will give Anthony and I a little bit of privacy, keeping us out of earshot of the bartender and other patrons.

"What can I get you?" the guy behind the counter asks.

"What do you have on tap?"

The bartender rattles off the list to me, and I settle on a local IPA from a microbrewery. When he hands me the beer and returns to the customers at the other end of the bar, I take a sip. What's the best way to bring up to Anthony that his mother wants to meet with him? Should I just blurt it out the moment he sits down next to me or should I ease into it first? The truth is I just don't know.

Seeing Anthony walk in through the front door, I feel my heart skip a beat. God, he looks so good in those tight jeans and black T-shirt. I would love to run up to him, wrap my arms around his muscled body, and plant a kiss on him. But instead, I wave him over, and as usual, we're just going to talk.

He walks over to me but doesn't sit down. "What's so damn important, Stephen?"

"You don't have to be an ass from the get-go, Anthony. I may not be on your top-ten list, but I'm not your doormat either. I deserve to be treated with a little respect."

"You're right." He takes a seat next to me. "I'm sorry, but I'm still curious as to what this is all about."

Okay. Just blurt it out, Stephen.

But before I can, the bartender returns.

"You're Tony 'The Beast,' aren't you?" The guy smiles.

"Yeah," he answers. "That's me."

"That's so cool. I've seen you fight. I'm a big fan. I'm Kevin."

"Hey, Kevin." He shakes his hand. "You already know my name."

"I sure do." Kevin looks at me and then at Anthony. "You looked great in the cage, but my seat was pretty far back the last time I saw you fight. I must say, you look really hot close up."

Anthony smiles back at him, making me feel a tinge of jealousy.

"Your first drink is on me."

"Thanks. I'll have a Jack on the rocks."

"Coming right up, Beast." He and Anthony laugh.

Though I'm glad for the bartender's remarks because it lightened the mood and broke Anthony's ice a bit, I'm really ready for him to return to the other end of the bar. It's pretty obvious that Kevin wants to be more than just Anthony's fan.

Kevin returns with Anthony's drink and passes him his phone number written on a napkin. "Call me sometime."

"Hey, buddy," I say, feeling the tinge explode into a full-on green-eyed tsunami. "We're good on drinks and would like a little privacy. We'll let you know if we need anything."

Kevin steps back, slinging a bar towel over his shoulder. "I'm sorry, fellas. I didn't know you were together."

"We're not a couple," Anthony shoots back. "But we are friends and would like some privacy."

"Sure thing, Tony." Kevin smiles, clearly happy to hear the news that we aren't together.

My reaction to Anthony's statement is quite the opposite. It pisses me off.

As Kevin walks away, I down the rest of my beer and slam the glass on the counter.

"What's the matter with you?" Anthony asks.

"You know damn well what's wrong with me. You're being a total prick. You know how I feel about you, and yet you have the audacity to flirt with that empty-headed idiot right in front of me."

"Hey, I didn't do anything wrong. Kevin was flirting with me."

"You made it quite clear that we're not a couple."

"Well, we're not. You made it quite clear that you didn't want me the other day."

"Don't play games with me, Anthony. You know exactly what I meant."

"I guess I do, but that doesn't change a thing." He takes a sip of Kevin's drink. "We're at a stalemate, Stephen. I'm okay moving to friends-with-bennies between us, but no more. You, on the other hand, want to zip to the fast lane and down the altar. We're on opposite sides and I don't see how that's going to change." Anthony's words feel like punches to my gut. "Is that why you asked me here? To see if you could convince me otherwise?"

"No, though I would like to talk about that too." I take a deep breath, trying to find a sliver of calm and to push back at the jealousy inside me. "You're right. I don't have any say on who you flirt with or hook up with or whatever. But if you care about me at all, please, don't rub my face in it."

He takes another drink from his glass. "And you're right, too. I was wrong to flirt with that guy in front of you."

"Then why did you do it? Didn't you know how that would make me feel? Are you actually interested in him?"

"Hell, no." He smiles. "It's just nice to be noticed. So what do you really want to talk about with me?"

"Give me a second." Even though I'd rather Kevin stay right where he is, I need another drink before I dive into the real reason we're here, so I motion to him to bring us another round.

This time when he delivers our drinks, Anthony doesn't give him any notice, which pleases me. Kevin returns to his customers at the other end of the bar.

I take a big gulp from my second beer. "It's about your mother, Anthony."

"My mother?" His unblinking eyes fix on me. "What about my mother? You don't even know her, and I haven't seen her in years."

"But Nicco has, and he took me to her house the other day."

"Why in the hell would he do that? He doesn't want anything to do with that bitch any more than I do." Anthony's body language is easy to read—folded arms, narrow eyes, and thinning lips. His walls are back up and in full force.

That bitch? Harsh words, but justified, given all he went through under Carlotta's roof. I've got my work cut out for me if I'm going to convince him to meet with her.

"You're wrong about Nicco, Anthony. He's been meeting with her for some time."

"Damn it. She's gotten her claws into him again."

"Your mother is in recovery, and she's been clean for over a year now. Somehow Nicco found it in his heart to forgive her."

"Of course he did," Anthony says with hatred in his eyes and sarcasm in his tone. "He better get ready for another big disappointment. I know her broken promises. I can't even count the number of times she told me she would quit and how much she loved me. And then, she went right back to the crack pipe. Stephen, her drugs are number one. Always. No matter what Nicco thinks, I'm sure she's getting high."

"I met her, Anthony. You would be surprised. Nicco says your mom is just like she was when you two were little and your dad was still alive." I see a slight shift in his body language, which gives me hope. "Recovery is hard, and most addicts do relapse. But not all of them, especially the ones who have people who care around them. She wants to see you. Nicco hasn't brought it up to you because he wasn't sure how you'd react."

"And that's why he brought you in to the equation, right? He thought I would listen to you more than him."

"I guess so." I place my hand over his, and he doesn't pull it back. Maybe I am getting through to him. "I can tell how difficult this is for you, and I don't blame you. But will you consider meeting with her at least for the memory of when you were little? Do you remember that far back?"

"Yes. I remember. I remember cupcakes…and birthdays…and she and Dad tucking me in at night." He downs the rest of his second drink. "What do you think kept me sane all those terrible years after my father died?" He laughs, obviously not from anything funny but from wounds and scars deep down inside him. "Sane? I'm not sane. You more than anyone know that."

"It's your choice whether to meet her or not. I'm just telling you what I saw in your mother when I met her. I'm no stranger to addicts and their games. In my opinion she's clean right now, but you can see for yourself if you so choose to."

Kevin walks up to us. "More drinks?"

Anthony ignores him, locking his eyes with mine. Then, to my surprise, he leans over and kisses me right in front of the empty-headed bartender. When he releases my lips, I am more in love with him than I ever have been.

I glance at Kevin, who has returned to the other end of the bar. Though his frown shouldn't please me, it does.

Anthony stands, placing some cash on the counter. "I need time to think about it."

I nod, finding it impossible to speak at the moment.

"You're the best," he says, as if we're still just friends.

"Uh, huh," is all I can verbalize.

He grins and gives me a hug, holding on tight for more than a minute. I'm so mixed up. I can't make heads or tails out of the signals he's giving me.

He releases me and walks out of the club.

Why didn't I tell him I needed a ride back to Mockingbird Place? Because I'm totally confused.

That kiss, that wonderful kiss. What did it mean?

Kevin walks up and takes the cash Anthony left. "Anything else?"

"No thanks." I bring out my phone to call for an Uber driver.

Are Anthony's walls coming down? Or am I just being a fool once again?

AS I FINISH my last cup of coffee before heading to the church, my phone buzzes. It's a text from Nicco.

"Bro and I had a long talk about our mom. He'll be at your door in 60 seconds."

I type back, *"Thanks for the heads up."*

No time to prepare for this one.

Knock. Knock.

I walk to the door, wondering if Anthony is or isn't going to meet with his mother. I guess I'm about to find out.

I open the door. "Hey. Come on in. I can put on a pot of coffee."

"No, thanks," he says, remaining on the other side of my door. "Besides, don't you have office hours at your church today?"

"Yes, I do, but I can flex my time when I need to. Do I need to?"

"Nope," he says flatly, which lets me know that his walls are back up and just as thick as ever.

The more walls he builds between us, the more I want to buy him an Erector Set. The thought makes me smile.

"What's so funny?" he asks.

"Nothing." *Mr. Wall Builder.* I try to keep from grinning but fail.

My smile seems to confuse Anthony.

Turnabout is fair play, isn't it? I was confused about his kiss last night. Hell, he's played hot and cold with me a million times, keeping me confused. This one time, he can be the one confused.

Broadening my smile, I say, "What can I do for you?"

"I've talked with Nicco and have agreed to meet our mother. He's calling her now about meeting tonight at seven."

"I'm glad, Anthony."

"No promises. I don't know how I feel about this or how I will react to seeing her again. I promised Nicco I would hear her out and try not to blow up."

"A good promise."

Suddenly, his walls seem to come down. "I'd like you to go with us. I need your moral support."

"Of course, I'll go. Where are you meeting her?"

"Her house. I want to see for myself if she's everything you and Nicco say she is. We're leaving at six."

"I'll be ready."

"I better go so you can get to your church and get to work." He grins. "Good-bye, Smiley Face."

I watch him turn around and head down the sidewalk to his apartment. He glances back at me and winks before going inside.

"Damn, he's got me hanging again. He always wins."

Chapter 18

I sit in the back on the drive to Carlotta's house. Nicco is driving, with Anthony in the passenger seat. We haven't said much since we left Mockingbird Place. The tension is building with every mile.

When we pull into her driveway, Anthony sighs. "At least she's got a good lawn service."

"Don't, bro," Nicco says. "Please, give her a chance. And besides, Mom is the one who keeps the yard mowed, not a service. Even the flowerbeds are her handiwork. You remember how much she loved gardening, don't you?"

"Of course I do. Let's get this over with."

I reach over the seat and place my hand on his shoulder. "Feel my moral support, Anthony. Just breathe. Okay?"

"Okay. I'll try." He takes a deep breath.

The three of us get out of the car. I'm a little stunned to see Anthony get to the door first and knock.

Nicco and I stand behind him.

The door opens.

Carlotta wraps her arms around Anthony and begins to sob. "I'm so sorry, Anthony. So sorry."

He doesn't hug her back. His arms remain at his sides.

She steps back, wiping her eyes.

Looking at Anthony's face, I can tell her attire is a shock to him. She's dressed in a pretty sundress and sandals. Her makeup is perfect, complementing her olive skin. Unlike before, she has her hair up in a ponytail.

She looks at Anthony. "I'm sorry for that. It's just when I saw you…I couldn't…it's so…" A nervous smile appears on her face. "Thank you for agreeing to see me. Please, come in. I have a batch of your favorite cookies that I just pulled out of the oven."

"You remember my favorite," he says flatly.

She flinches slightly at his tone. "Peanut butter, right?"

"Right." He walks past her like a soldier heading to the front lines.

This isn't going to be easy for any of us, but especially Anthony. *Please God. Please.*

Nicco and I sit on the sofa, just like we did the other day. Anthony takes the seat Carlotta had sat in.

She remains standing. "There are plenty of cookies for each of you. What would you like to drink? I have milk, coffee, and—"

"How about a beer?" Anthony shoots back in a rough tone. "Or a whiskey?"

"I don't have any of that in my house, Anthony," she says meekly. "Nicco did tell you that I'm in recovery, didn't he?"

"That's what *he* said." Anthony's tone remains harsh, with a razor-sharp edge that cuts to the core.

"Anthony!" Nicco is clearly agitated at the direction this meeting is taking. "Don't be an ass."

No one says a word, and Carlotta seems frozen in place, not sure what to do next.

"I'll have coffee with my cookies, if you don't mind," I say to her, hoping to alleviate some of the tension in the room.

Nicco smiles. "Me, too."

"Same." Anthony sighs.

Thankfully, I can tell the tension has eased up a bit, like a teapot letting off some steam. But I suspect that underneath Anthony's hard exterior is a sea of churning emotions—more like a massive pressure cooker than a tiny teapot.

Carlotta hurries into the kitchen.

I watch Anthony study the neat and clean surroundings. Is he coming to the same conclusion I did when I first came here? His mom's recovery is going extremely well. But does that matter to him? Can he forgive her? After all that happened, I just don't know.

She returns with our coffee and cookies and takes the seat next to Anthony. She looks him straight in the eyes. "I don't expect you to forgive me. I just needed to tell you how sorry I am, but I know that words aren't enough for all the pain I brought you. I'm so ashamed."

For the first time since I've known Anthony, I can tell he doesn't know what to say. Whenever I've seen him with his back against one of his walls and someone threatening to bring them down, he lashes out and then walks away.

I watch the two of them—mother and son—just stare at each other. I glance at Nicco, who seems as at a loss of what to do next as I am. Nervous energy pushes me to take a bite of one of Carlotta's cookies.

This silence is killing me. Please, one of you say something!

But the crushing quiet remains.

When I can't take another second of it, I say, "These cookies are really good, Carlotta."

Everyone turns to me with baffled looks on their faces.

"What?" Nicco asks.

"Well, don't you think these cookies are good?" I know I'm digging my hole even deeper, but I just can't stop myself. "They've got to be the best I've ever had, and I've had a lot of cookies. And that coffee. Wow. Carlotta, do you grind your own beans?"

Anthony starts laughing, and we all join in until tears are rolling out of our eyes.

When we settle down, he looks at his mother. "I know that Nicco has forgiven you, but I'm not there yet. I don't know if I'll ever be, but I will hear you out."

"That's more than I ever dreamed of, Anthony. I don't expect you to ever forgive me or even to think of me as your mother. I'm just so thrilled to have a chance to see you again. Thank you from the bottom of my heart."

ON THE WAY back to Mockingbird Place, I sense a change in Anthony. I've never heard him so chatty before. I love hearing all the stories about him and Nicco growing up with their dad and mom. It sounds like a veritable heaven on earth back then.

"Nicco, remember when Dad built that tree house in the back-yard for us? It was like a castle in the sky. You climbed up that ladder like a monkey, and I stood at the bottom crying, scared to death to go up."

Nicco nods. "I remember. Didn't Dad piggyback you up the ladder?"

"He sure did. Even though I was scared out of my mind, I held on as tight as I could. And guess what? It was all worth it." He looks over his shoulder at me. "From then on I was able to climb up and down the ladder all by myself."

"I bet you were a handful at that age," I say with a grin.

"I was. " His tone is very quiet, almost a whisper. He glances down at the sack of peanut butter cookies his mother gave him before we left. "Our mom always made sure there were plenty of cookies for us whenever Dad, Nicco, and I were in that tree house."

I can tell he's struggling, remembering the boy he was and the mother Carlotta was before his father died.

The last few miles, none of us say a word.

I decide it might be best to invite them over to my place. "Hey, guys. How about we have a beer together before we call it a night? I've got a six-pack in my fridge."

"I'm for that," Nicco says. "How about you, bro?"

"Yeah. I could definitely use a beer."

After Nicco parks his car, we get out and walk to my apartment.

"Come on in, guys. Have a seat. I'll get the beer."

Nicco and Anthony sit down at my kitchen table. After I hand them a bottle, I sit down with one of my own.

"She did look nice," Anthony says. "And the house looked nice. The cookies tasted good. But I don't know if I can ever forgive her, let alone trust her." He looks at Nicco. "How did you do it? It's her fault you were in prison all those years. Hers and mine."

"Your fault?" Nicco shakes his head. "Why would you think that?"

Anthony takes a drink of his beer before answering. "You went to prison because of me. If you hadn't seen that fucker on top of me, you would have remained free."

Nicco reaches across the table and grabs Anthony's hand. "You're my brother. I had to protect you. It wasn't your fault. Remember, the gang, *my gang* killed him. I just took the blame, and none of those sorry assholes ever stepped up to clear my name. Code of silence."

"Yeah, but Mom could have done something. Instead, she just kept her mouth shut and remained in her drug-induced haze."

"Hey, you don't know her whole story. Hell, I didn't know it until I took Stephen with me the other day to her house."

"What story are you talking about?"

Nicco tells him about their mother's horrific childhood, about being locked in a closet for days, and so much more. "Dad saved her from a terrible life, Anthony. We couldn't see how fragile she was. We were just kids. But when Dad died, her whole world and foundation was destroyed."

"That's no excuse, Nicco. She was our mother. We needed her."

I lean forward. "That's almost exactly what Carlotta told me the day I met her. After she shared her story, she admitted that she had no excuses."

Nicco nods. "Mom knows that nothing that happened to her is any excuse for what happened to you and me. She can't forgive herself, bro. I doubt she'll ever be able to. Nothing you or I can do will punish her any more than she's already suffered. But what you should know is she wasn't capable of helping us. She couldn't even help herself."

"But we're the ones who have suffered, Nicco. You and I. I wish I could feel the way you do about her, but I doubt I ever will."

He glances at the bag of cookies, like they're some kind of talisman that has the power over time itself. In a way, it does. I can see that he's back in that tree house in his mind, his dad piggy-backing him up and down the ladder and his mom bringing out a fresh batch of peanut butter cookies.

Nicco looks at me, as if imploring me for answers. But I really don't have any. This is Anthony's journey.

He turns back to Anthony. "Would you consider going with Mom to one of her meetings? I did and it really opened my eyes."

"I don't know. Maybe."

"Whatever you decide, Anthony, I would like to put you both in touch with a friend of mine who works with Nar-Anon." I bring out my phone to get the contact. "It's a support group for friends and family of addicts. I really believe it would be beneficial."

Anthony blows out a bunch of air. "I'll think about it. Thanks, Stephen, for the beer and for everything."

"I'm glad to have helped, no matter how small it is."

He stands, and Nicco and I also come to our feet.

"You both have given me a lot to think about. I need to sleep on it. Goodnight, Stephen."

"Goodnight," I say.

Nicco tells me "goodnight" and follows him out my front door. As I watch them walk down the sidewalk to Unit J, I pray that Anthony will find some peace through all of this.

Please, God. Help him.

Whether Anthony forgives his mother or not, I will do all in my power to help him.

Chapter 19

I smile at my favorite vestry member, sitting on the other side of my desk. "Mrs. Clark, I can honestly say I've never met a more organized or capable person in my life. Looks like you have everything under control for the mission trip to Mexico. Good job."

"Thank you, Father." She smiles, gathering up her folders.

My phone buzzes. It's a text from Anthony.

"What a wonderful smile. Is that your special someone?" she asks with a grin. "I don't mean to be nosy. But a happy rector makes for a happy parish."

"Well in that case, it is someone special."

"I knew it. I knew it. I knew it." She claps her hands. "Does he have a name?" She covers her mouth with her hands. "That is being too nosy, isn't it?"

"It's okay. His name is Anthony."

"That's a wonderful name. So when you decide to get married, I expect you to call on me to help. You did say I was the most organized and capable person you've ever met. And I just love weddings."

"We're not even dating yet," I tell her. "And I'm not sure he's the marrying kind."

"Well, if he doesn't want to marry someone as wonderful and handsome as you, let me have a talk with him. I'll know what to say." She winks. "I'm good at that even more than being organized."

"I bet you are."

I'm not sure why I'm divulging so much about my personal life. Maybe it's because I find it so easy to talk to this wonderful woman. No judgment. Just kindness and love. I wonder what she would say to Anthony if she ever met him.

I glance down at my phone, as another text comes in from Anthony. I'm anxious to read both of them.

"At best, a wedding will still be quite some time, if that ever happens. But I promise I'll call you if things change and we decide to get married."

She stands and extends her hand across the desk. "It's a deal."

I come around and give her a hug. "Yes, it is."

I walk with her to my office door.

Another text causes my phone to buzz.

"Seems like your Anthony is very excited about something." She grins. "It's a good thing I'm your last appointment today. Gives you time alone to text him back. Good-bye, Father."

"Good-bye, Mrs. Clark." I go back to my desk to read Anthony's text messages.

"Stephen, thanks again. Nicco and I did contact Nar-Anon. We're headed to a meeting right now."

"That's great news," I say aloud and read the second text message.

"I'm not sure if I'm ready to go with my mother to one of her meetings yet. We'll see. Baby steps."

Better to think it through, but I'm glad he's considering it.

"Can I come over after the Nar-Anon meeting?"

My heart jumps in my chest. Is the hard shell around Anthony cracking? I hope so.

I quickly text back, *"Please come over. I'd love to hear about the meeting. I'll order pizza."*

"Great. See you at 7."

THE PIZZA DELIVERY guy just left. Knowing Anthony's favorite is pepperoni and that he usually has a big appetite, I ordered two larges.

My doorbell rings, and I quickly look around the room to make sure everything is perfect. Pizza is on the table. The bottle of wine is open. Music is playing softly in the background. Even though tonight isn't really a date with Anthony, I want to make sure it's special.

I open the door and smile at him. He looks good enough to eat in his boots, jeans, and pullover. "Come on in. Hope you're hungry. I ordered a large pizza for each of us."

"Starving," he says and gives me a hug.

"Let's go sit down." I lead him to the table and pour each of us a glass of wine.

"If I didn't know better, Father Stephen, I would think you were trying to seduce me. Candles. Music. Wine. And you're looking mighty fine." He grins.

Damn. Did I go overboard? But seeing that wicked smile makes me think he's okay with it.

"I don't know if I would call it an act of seduction. I just wanted to make it special for us. It's been a long time since we had dinner here." I hold up my glass. "And by the way, you're *looking mighty fine* too. Cheers to both of us."

He clinks his glass to mine. "Cheers."

"How did it go at the meeting tonight?" I ask as we both grab a slice of pizza.

"Very enlightening. I really learned a lot, which I wasn't expecting. I even learned a lot about myself."

"Really? Like what?"

"There were about fifteen people in the meeting, and they reminded me of Nicco and me. They all shared how dealing with their individual family or friend's addiction impacted them. We heard lots of heartbreaking stories. I thought Nicco and I suffered more than anyone, but I found out that isn't true. One woman lost her two kids in a single night to heroin. Now she's alone. I at least have Nicco and we haven't lost our mother yet."

"Did going to the meeting help you?"

"Yeah, it did. The group helped me see that addiction is a disease, not a weakness of character. I never looked at it that way. My mom has an illness. I can't change that, but I can try to understand."

"You got all that from one meeting?"

He grins. "Malcolm always told me I was a fast learner. I guess he was right."

"He was right. Have you made up your mind if you're going to see your mom again?"

"I have. Nicco and I will be going with her to one of her meetings. It's a baby step for me, but at least it's a first step. I have a lot more to learn. They have a 12-step program that I'm going to use in my day-to-day life. So is Nicco. He and I are going to start attending the meeting every week. Thank you for suggesting it."

"You're welcome. I'm so proud of you. This is hard work, but if anyone can do it, it's you." I clear the table. "How about we take our wine into the living room?"

"Perfect." He sits down on the sofa.

It might be better for me to sit in the chair opposite the sofa, but I want to be close to him. Foolish? Probably. Still, I can't resist and sit right next to him.

Is it the wine or the music that brings the memory of him telling me he loved me into my mind? Maybe neither. Maybe it's just my own desires that have brought it out again. I've thought about it at least a thousand times since it happened. And like every time before, I remind myself that Anthony was in a hospital bed filled with drugs when he said those three words to me.

"This has been great, Stephen." His eyes lock with mine. "I've missed this. I've missed you."

"Me, too. I'd like more nights like this."

"So would I, but—"

"But what? We're good together, and you know how I feel about you."

"That's the point," he says. "You're pushing really hard for something I'm not sure is possible between us."

"And you've been pushing me for sex without any commitment. I want the forever."

He smiles. "You're not like most guys, that's for sure."

"You're right. I am different."

"Is it because you're a priest?"

"No. I'm flesh and blood just like anyone else. I just need more. You know about my past, my childhood. I've been alone my whole life. No family. I want that. I want that with you."

"But how can that work? You're a priest, and I don't believe in God."

"So? That doesn't matter. I can't judge you or anyone else. Everyone's path is different. Maybe someday you will believe, but if you don't that won't change my love for you. Anthony, can't you believe in us?"

He doesn't say anything but just keeps looking at me.

Those damn walls of his. Will they ever come down? "Say something."

"I know I want you, Stephen. But that's all I have for now."

Is that the problem? Have I come on so strong that he can't help but bring up his defenses?

"What if we go slow?" I ask him. "Just go on a date. Nothing fancy. We could take it one step at a time. See what happens."

He grins. "You're unrelenting and stubborn."

"I told you that I was never giving up." I take his hand, and to my utter thrill, he doesn't take it back. God, I want him to kiss me more than anything right now. Why can't I kiss him?

I lean in close and press my lips to his. Anthony deepens our kiss, and I feel heat roll through me. "I love you so much."

"Damn it, Stephen." He leaps from the sofa. "Why did you say that to me? This is your idea of taking it slow? One step at a time? You just don't get it, do you? I want your body, but I don't want your love."

I know he loves me. I've seen it in his eyes a million times. But he can't admit that to me or to himself. "It's time for you to leave, Anthony. We're obviously not on the same page."

"Obviously. Thanks for dinner." He rushes out the door.

I pound my fist on the table. "Why did I say it?"

It was a mistake. I know that now. I got caught up in the moment and it just came out. And now everything is back to the way it was, with us further apart than before.

"Damn!"

HOW LONG HAVE I been staring at the ceiling? I roll over in my bed and glance at the clock.

3:44 a.m.

No sense in just lying here. I'm not going to get any sleep. My mind keeps replaying my last argument with Anthony. I need some sort of distraction. I could work on my sermon for Sunday. I can see the title now. "Don't tell someone you love them. It might ruin your life." Guess I'm not really in the right frame of mind.

My phone rings.

I sit up on the side of my bed and see that it's Anthony calling. I can feel my entire body tense. "Anthony, it's late. What do you want?"

"Stephen, I need you."

Chapter 20

"What did you say, Anthony?" I ask, completely confused.

"I need you," he repeats in an anxious tone. "Martha collapsed and fell down the stairs. Sarah called us, and then I called you. Jaris and Maddox are already here and the ambulance is on the way."

"I'll be right there." I leap from the bed, get dressed, and head out the door. *Please God. Please.*

Every light is on in Unit I, where S & M live, and I hear the sirens of the ambulance approaching. The front door is open, so I walk inside.

Martha is unconscious and on the floor at the foot of the stairs. She's wearing her nightgown. She must have gotten out of bed for some reason and fallen then. Jaris and Maddox are on either side of her, checking her vitals. I never realized how lucky we are to have two doctors living at Mockingbird Place.

Nicco comes down the stairs with a blanket. "I found one." He covers Martha with it.

"Is she going to be okay?" I ask them.

"Not sure yet," Jaris says. "Doesn't look like she broke any bones, but her heart rate is very slow and erratic and her temperature is low."

Maddox looks at me. "We need to get her to the hospital quickly."

Nicco points to the kitchen at Sarah and Anthony. "They need you, Father Stephen."

Sarah is beside herself, sobbing. Anthony is holding her, but he's also very upset and clearly unable to console her.

I walk into the kitchen and put my arms around both of them. "Martha is in good hands, and you both know how strong she is."

Sarah leans her head into my chest. "I can't lose her. I'd be lost without her, Stephen."

In these situations, I've seen how loved ones can feel powerless and lost. What's worked for me in the past to calm nerves is to remind them of something familiar that they can do. I hope it will work for Sarah and Anthony. "Martha is a strong woman. She's going to be okay. Let's all pray. 'Our Father, who art in heaven…' "

Sarah repeats the Lord's Prayer with me. Anthony remains silent, holding her hand. At the end, I add a personal prayer for dear Martha.

With tears still in her eyes, a calmer Sarah says, "Thank you, Stephen. You don't know what it means to me that you're here with us."

"Thank you so much for coming." Anthony places his hand on my shoulder. "We definitely need you right now."

Funny what a difference there is between how Anthony and I left each other last night and now. When something like this happens, everyone has to pull together. We were both defensive in our own way. But right now, all that matters is Martha.

The EMTs rush in and Jaris and Maddox fill them in on Martha's condition. When they are loading her into the ambulance, as usual, all of our neighbors are gathered together to offer their help. I ask them to pray.

"I'd like to ride with you," Sarah says to the EMTs.

"I'm sorry, ma'am, but in this situation our rules don't allow it."

"Let her go with you." Maddox isn't taking no for an answer. "I'll be responsible."

"Okay, Doc," one of them says, helping Sarah climb into the back of the ambulance.

I turn to Nicco and Anthony. "I'll drive you two. Besides, I always have a parking space right up front. Come on."

Nicco gets in my back seat, and Anthony takes the passenger seat next to me. I turn on my flashers and stay right behind the ambulance.

When we get inside the ER, I recognize the woman behind the desk. "Hi, Lela."

"Hello, Father."

"Do you know what room they took Ms. Rivers to?"

"Room seven, but she's on her way to X-ray right now. Her wife is in the room though."

"Thank you." I lead Anthony and Nicco through the double doors to room seven.

Sarah is talking with an admission clerk, who has a rolling computer desk. "Oh God, I didn't bring her Medicare card."

The three of us surround her.

"It's okay, S," Anthony says. "We'll figure this out. It's going to be fine."

The admitting clerk nods. "Ma'am, has she ever been in this hospital before?"

"Just for tests," Sarah tells her.

"Good. Then she's already in our system. What's her name and birthdate?"

Sarah rattles the information off to her.

"Here she is." The clerk smiles. "Like your son said, everything is just fine. When you're able, bring in her ID, Medicare card, and any supplemental insurance she has."

"I will. Thank you so much for your help."

As the clerk is leaving, she says, "It's my pleasure to help you."

"Boys, please remind me about getting those things later." Sarah sighs. "I'm not sure I'll remember."

"How about I go back to your apartment and get all the documents that clerk wants and whatever else you need?" I ask.

"That would be wonderful."

Anthony turns to Nicco. "Would you mind going with Stephen? I left my phone in our apartment, and I need to call Sam to cancel my fight tomorrow."

I'm not surprised that Anthony's priority is only about S & M right now. His career is a distant second.

"Of course, I'll go," Nicco says.

"Anthony, you can use mine to call Sam." I hold out my phone to him.

"Unfortunately, I don't remember his number," Anthony says. "Hell, I don't remember anyone's. I always rely on my contact list."

"Me, too." I turn to Sarah. "Do you have your phone?"

She pulls it and her keys out of her purse. "Yes. Anthony or I will call you if they bring M back from X-ray or we get any news." Sarah hands me her key. "Martha's purse is on the dresser in our bedroom."

"We'll be right back."

When Nicco and I rush back through the ER double doors, we find all our neighbors sitting in the waiting area. When they see us, they jump up and everyone starts asking questions at once.

Trace holds up his hand. "One at a time, folks."

Everyone quiets down.

"Any news about Martha?" he asks. "We're all very concerned."

"All we know is they took her back to X-ray," I say.

"And how is Sarah?"

"She's doing as best as she can. Anthony is with her."

"How's he doing?" Oliver asks.

"He's holding up." Nicco is a big, tough guy, but his voice cracks with emotion. "But it's hard for my brother. Each of you know how much S & M mean to him."

Adam, who is tough himself being a former Marine, puts his arm around Nicco. "We're here for him and S & M, my friend. And you, too."

"I know. Thanks."

"We have to run back to the apartment," I tell my wonderful neighbors. "Has anyone called Harvey?"

"I have," Trace says. "He and Nathan are on their way."

"Good. If you hear anything while we're gone, please call us."

Trace nods. "Sure thing, Stephen."

On the way back to Mockingbird Place, Nicco asks, "What's going on between you and Anthony? When he came home last night he was in a foul mood. He slammed the refrigerator door so hard he turned over a bottle of wine that went everywhere. I thought about offering to help him clean up the mess but decided not to. I'm pretty sure he would have bit off my head if I had."

"Sounds like you got the fallout from our argument. Our time together didn't go as I had planned, obviously. We were doing just fine until I decided to kiss him."

"What could go wrong with a kiss? I know Anthony is crazy about you."

"I'm crazy about him and I feel like he cares about me too. But he's not ready for a relationship. He's made that very clear to me. He only wants a friends-with-benefits arrangement, and I just can't do that. I need much more than that. I'm not asking for a ring on my finger right now, but I have to at least believe that we are moving in the same direction."

"Please, don't give up on my brother. He just needs more time."

"I won't, but I'm not sure that even with more time anything will change. His wounds are deep, Nicco."

"I know they are. The hell he's been through has wrecked him."

"No wonder he doesn't want a relationship with me or anyone else. He doesn't trust anybody, and he definitely doesn't believe in forever. Why should he? After your dad died his whole world fell apart and eventually he lost everyone he loved. Your mother. Even you, when you went to prison."

"If he could only work out things with Mom, it would be a start."

"Well, at least he's trying. But you and I know that's going to take a lot of effort. I'm glad you two went to the Nar-Anon meeting."

"Me, too. Anthony isn't the only one with demons to exercise." Nicco points at his own chest. "I've done a ton of things I'm not proud of."

"So have I." The image of Father O'Malley's bashed car windows burns in the back of my mind. "But we can't beat ourselves up forever, Nicco. We have to move on and do better."

He nods. "I'm just worried that something horrible might happen to Martha. If, God forbid, it does, Anthony may slip backward to a dark place that none of us can pull him out of."

"You're forgetting how strong Martha is, and don't underestimate your brother like that. He's also stronger than we can imagine."

"I know he's stronger than I am. I believe that with all my heart."

"If your brother and I ever have a chance of being together, I have to believe that too." I turn my car into the complex's parking lot. "I asked Anthony if he could believe in us."

"What did he say?"

"He didn't answer. But I'm not going to stop believing or hoping. No matter how long I have to wait, I want him in my life. Forever."

Chapter 21

After getting Martha's purse and Anthony's phone, Nicco and I head back to the hospital in my car.

"Stephen, you know how S & M always take care of everyone whenever there's a crisis?"

"I sure do." I turn left at the next intersection. "I'm pretty sure they're actually angels in disguise."

"We need to take over angelic duties for them. Do you mind stopping at the bakery on Cedar Springs so we can get some donuts for the gang?"

"That's a great idea, Nicco."

Once we're at the bakery's counter, he orders two-dozen glazed donuts and three-dozen of several varieties.

Remembering what Anthony's favorites are, I add to the baker, "Could you give me a half-dozen chocolate icing with sprinkles?"

When we get back to the hospital all the parking spaces are taken, including the two clergy spots next to the ER entrance.

"I guess we'll have to park in the remote lot across the street."

Nicco and I walk into the ER waiting area with five-dozen donuts and the half-dozen I got for Anthony.

"Any news about Martha?" I ask Trace.

"Not yet, but Anthony came out about five minutes ago. He asked me to send both of you to Martha's room once you arrived. They're expecting news any minute."

Nicco places the five-dozen donuts on the coffee table, and I keep hold of the donuts I got for Anthony.

We walk through the double doors and come face to face with the attendant, who is pushing the gurney with Martha on it down the hall. I'm thrilled to see her sitting up.

She turns to Nicco and me.

Her left eye is sporting quite the shiner. "Guys, where's S?"

"She's with Anthony in the last room down that hall," Nicco tells her. "You're heading there now."

"I can't wait to see her. She needs to know that I'm fine."

I never cease being amazed at S & M's relationship. Their love for each other is an example for all of us. "Jaris and Maddox must have done their doctor magic on you because you look good."

"I guess their magic is in whatever is in my IV." She points at the IV bag that is attached to the line in the back of her hand. "Jaris told me I would feel so much better once I got some fluids in me. This is my second bag, and I feel great."

Nicco holds the door for the attendant, who wheels Martha and her bed into the room.

Sarah and Anthony jump to their feet.

"Oh, my sweet baby," Sarah says with a wide grin. "You look so great, other than that shiner, which you clearly got from your fall."

"I've never had a black eye before. Honey, give me a mirror. I've got to see it."

Sarah pulls out a compact from her purse and hands it to Martha.

Martha looks at her reflection in the tiny mirror. She giggles. "My goodness, that's a doozy. Somebody take a picture. I want evidence."

"I'll do it," Anthony says, snapping a photo of her with his phone. "I'll send it to you right now."

"I want a copy," Nicco says.

I nod. "Me, too."

"Anthony, send it to everyone." Martha grins and hands the compact back to Sarah. "Maybe I'll get more sympathy flowers, and you know how I love flowers."

"You're a mess, baby." Sarah leans over and kisses her on the forehead. "You were gone a long time, M. What tests did they run on you back there?"

"Got a good checking over, I'll tell you that. They ran so many tests, my new nickname is 'pin cushion,' sweetheart."

We laugh, and Sarah says, "How about I call you 'pin' for short?"

"S, just please keep calling me M, okay?"

"You know I will," she says softly.

After the attendant finishes hooking Martha back up to the monitors, Jaris and Maddox walk into the room.

"What is this?" Maddox smiles. "A party?"

"You bet it is," Martha says. "And I'm the guest of honor."

Jaris nods. "You sure are. You gave us quite the scare, young lady, but the good news is you don't have any broken bones and should be back on your feet in no time at all."

"What caused this, Jaris?" Sarah grabs Martha's hand.

"Her blood work showed that her electrolytes were extremely low—especially her potassium. But this little cocktail that Maddox and I ordered for her will get all her electrolytes back to normal. As you can see, she already feels better."

Anthony takes Martha's other hand and looks at Jaris and Maddox. "Why would her potassium and other electrolytes be so low? Is this something we need to worry about?"

Maddox's eyebrows rise and he looks at Martha. "Do you want to tell them or shall Jaris and I?"

"I had a little upset stomach. That's all. I didn't feel like eating."

"How did you manage to keep that from me, M?"

"I didn't want to worry you and you know what a good actress I am."

"Apparently, Martha has been dealing with this for over a week," Jaris says. "She admitted she hasn't been eating since Stephen's Get Out Of Jail party."

Martha shrugs. "No big deal."

"No big deal?" Sarah looks at her sternly. "Look where you ended up. I had no idea you were that sick. You should have told me. You ever pull this again with me, M, and you know what kind of hell I will be dishing out to you." Sarah's words are firm, though I can tell from her tone that she's really relieved.

We all are, including Anthony.

"I hate to leave, but I really need to go. Since you're doing so well, I'm going to keep my meeting with the vestry at the church."

"Stephen, would you mind saying a prayer before you go?" Nicco asks.

Anthony nods. "I'm sure S & M would like that."

"We sure would," Martha says. "Right, S?"

She smiles. "You're right as rain, M. Will you, Stephen?"

"Of course I will." I ask God for a quick and full recovery for Martha. "Through Jesus Christ our Lord. Amen."

"Amen," S & M and Nicco say in unison.

"Thank you, Stephen." Sarah's eyes start to well up.

"What she said," Martha chokes out. "I don't know what else to say."

"You don't have to say anything. We're family."

"We sure are," Anthony says. "That's a fact."

I know what I mean when I say that we're family, but what does he mean? Sure, S & M are his family. Nicco, too. But how does he see me after all that has happened? I wonder.

Those questions will have to wait to be answered

I look at Anthony and Nicco. "I was your ride to the hospital. Should I take one of you back to the complex to get a car before I go to my meeting, or can you wait until I come back to check on Martha?"

"We can wait," Nicco says. "And if we need a ride, I'm sure Harvey or someone else will help us."

"Okay. Call if you need me."

Anthony smiles, and I feel my heart soar. "We will."

I walk to the door.

"Hold up, Stephen," he says. "I'll walk you out."

"I'd like that."

He kisses both S & M on the cheek and follows me out.

"That was some night we just went through," Anthony says. "Tougher than any match I've ever been in, that's for sure."

"But just like you, Martha came up the champ."

"She sure did."

We walk into the waiting area and Anthony fills in our neighbors about how well Martha is doing. They are thrilled to hear the news.

Seeing that the donuts Nicco and I brought are nearly gone, I realize I've been holding the box of donuts I got for Anthony—chocolate icing with sprinkles—the entire time.

"Come on, Stephen," Anthony says, heading to the exit. "You don't want to be late for your meeting."

"I won't be. I've got enough time to get there." I follow him out the door.

He glances at the two clergy spots, which are now empty. "Where are you parked?"

"Across the street. Those spaces were taken when Nicco and I got here." I hand him the donuts as we head to the crosswalk. "These are for you."

He opens the box, and his eyes light up like a kid opening a present at Christmas. "Chocolate icing with sprinkles."

"I know you like them and I also know how hard the last several hours have been on you."

"Thank you."

"You're welcome."

It's so good to be talking with him like this. It feels comfortable between us again. But is it really?

He hits the button for the crosswalk and then extends his hand to shake mine. "Thank you, Stephen. You're a good friend."

Something inside me cracks wide open and releases all of the frustration that I've been holding back for the past few weeks. "Are you fucking kidding me?"

His eyes widen and he pulls his hand back. "Stephen, I've never heard you use that word before."

"Well, you better get used to it because that's how the fuck I feel.

What the fuck do you mean calling me a good friend? Oh, my! There's that word again," I blurt out sarcastically. "A fucking hand-shake? Damn, Anthony, you sure do know how to cut me to the core. Friends? Is that all we are? Is that all we'll ever be?"

"Stephen, you don't under——"

"Oh, yes I do understand. I understand you perfectly. You want a fuck buddy. That's all I am to you. Just get one fucking thing straight. I love you. I will always love you. But I'm not putting up with your fucking bullshit any longer." I realize I'm out of control. "I have to get away from you right now."

I step off the curb and the sound of screeching brakes echoes in my ears. Looking to my left, I see the bus and hear Anthony screaming my name.

Chapter 22

nthony

"STEPHEN!" I scream.

In a fraction of a second the bus slams into Stephen, sending him flying in the air. He lands with a loud, horrible thud on the pavement fifteen feet away.

"Don't die, Stephen!" I run to him. "Please, don't die! Someone get help!"

I lean down next to him. His face is covered in blood.

"I'm here, sweetheart."

He doesn't respond and isn't moving.

"I'm sorry." I lightly touch his hand.

STEPHEN

. . .

I TRUDGE through a long dark tunnel, trying to reach the light at the very end. When I get closer, I see Father O'Malley and his wife, Ellen. They are dressed in white and look younger than I remember them. I'm filled with a sense of utter peace and joy.

"I thought you were dead," I say, continuing to approach them.

"Please, Stephen. Please. Hang on." Anthony's voice sounds so far away.

Anthony

"I CAN'T LOSE YOU. I've been so wrong."

The shaken bus driver comes up next to me. "He ran out in front of me. I'm so sorry. I had the green light."

His words are meaningless to me. All I care about is Stephen.

"Help is coming," the driver says. "I see them."

I glance over my shoulder and see some hospital staff running in our direction with a gurney.

"Please, step back, sir," the nurse tells me.

I nod, though I hate to put any distance between Stephen and me. "Please don't let him die."

"We'll do all we can for your friend," she says.

Friend? That's what I called him before he stepped off the curb. It's all my fault.

"Is he…is he alive?" I ask, fearing what the answer might be.

"Yes, he's still alive."

As she and the other staff carefully place Stephen's injured body on the gurney, my gut tightens, my knees go weak, and my mind swirls with a million things I should have already said to him. But I just pushed him away. Again and again.

Oh, God, what if I lose him? What if I never get the chance to tell him how much I love him?

The bus driver starts to say the Lord's Prayer. I remember believing in those words when I was just a boy. I'm not sure why I repeat the prayer with the bus driver now, especially since I don't believe in God. "But deliver us from evil," I whisper, feeling my heart seize in my chest.

If only those words were true.

In a complete daze, I follow the staff through the parking lot to the ER as the police arrive. The scene is chaotic.

"What's your friend's name?" the nurse asks me as we pass the double doors.

"Stephen. Stephen Norelli."

Her eyes widen. "Father Stephen?"

"Yes. Please let Dr. Jaris Black and Dr. Maddox Butler know. They're his friends and are in room number seven back there."

"I sure will let them know."

As we pass the waiting area, I hear Oliver call my name.

"Tony, what's going on?"

"Stephen. It's Stephen."

"What's happening with Stephen?" Harvey asks, as he and some of our neighbors rush out of the waiting area to me and Stephen's gurney.

"Oh, my God. Is that him?" Nathan says.

I close my eyes. "It's all my fault."

"Please step back," the nurse tells us. "We'll let you know as soon as we can about Father Stephen's condition."

She and the other staff members wheel Stephen to the back.

Harvey puts his arms around me. "Come with us, Tony."

I sit in one of the chairs, lost, terrified, and unable to speak. *Please, don't die.*

My friends surround me, and Nathan brings me a glass of water.

I drink it down and hand the empty glass back to him.

"Everybody, please back up and give Tony some breathing room," Harvey says. "Give him some space."

They all step back, but I know how much they care. I try to explain to them what happened without losing it. I'm honest and tell them about the fight Stephen and I had. "He was so mad at me that he walked right in front of the bus. So you see, it is all my fault."

"It isn't your fault just because you had a fight, Tony," Adam says, putting his arm around Oliver. "Fights happen between people who care about each other. This was just a terrible accident. Nothing more."

"I know you're trying to be kind, Adam, but I also know that it *is* my fault. And what if…what if Stephen doesn't make it? How will I ever be able to live with myself?"

Nicco rushes into the waiting room. "Anthony?"

When I see my brother I can't hold the tears back any longer and cover my face with my hands.

"He's over here, Nicco," Oliver tells him.

My brother takes the seat next to me and puts his arm around my shoulder.

I look at him. "I've been so wrong, so very wrong."

"Don't beat yourself up, bro. Stephen is in good hands. Jaris and Maddox are working with the ER doctors right now. They said that once they know more, one of them will come here to tell us. Stephen is going to be all right. We have to believe that."

"I'm trying," I say, though the image of Stephen's face covered in blood burns hot in my mind.

I look down at my feet, trying to keep from screaming.

"What can we do for you, Tony?" Trace asks me in a quiet tone. "Whatever you need, just say the word."

"Will you call Father Grissom and ask him to pray? I don't know if it will do any good, but I'm sure Stephen would want him too."

"And I'll call Stephen's church," Nicco says. "I'm sure they're wondering why he didn't make that meeting."

"Are you hungry?" Oliver asks.

"No, I'm not hungry," I snap back, and instantly wish I could take it back. "I'm sorry. I don't mean to be an asshole, but I just don't feel like talking."

He nods. "It's okay, Tony. I'm sure I would feel the same way."

"Thanks." I don't deserve to have such wonderful friends, but I'm glad I have them.

For the next hour and a half I keep looking at the time on my phone, feeling more and more helpless, anxious, and lost with each passing minute. "What the fuck is going on back there?"

Fuck. That's a word I never heard Stephen say before until we walked out of the ER. It's not like him, but I pushed him to it. Me. I'm the one to blame.

To all our surprise, S & M walk into the waiting room.

"What's going on?" I ask, rushing to them. "Martha, you were supposed to stay overnight."

"Do you think I was going to wait in a hospital room with our precious Stephen in surgery? I told Maddox I was fine, which I am, and I needed to be with you." She wraps her arms around me and I melt into her embrace. "Sweetheart, S and I are here."

Sarah wraps her arms around both of us. "It's going to be okay, son."

Once again, I feel the tears fall from my eyes. "Why couldn't I tell him I love him?"

Jackson stands at the entrance of the waiting area, looking down the hallway. "Here comes Maddox."

We break apart, anxious to hear the news.

Maddox walks straight to me. "Stephen is in surgery right now. Jaris is assisting. There are several things we have to fix. He has a broken arm and three broken ribs. But our two main concerns are his head injury and a piece of metal that is lodged in his neck near his spine. The CT scan showed that his brain is swelling from the trauma. Luckily for us, one of the best neurosurgeons in the country, Dr. Wilkinson, is on staff at the hospital. He may have to perform a ventriculostomy to relieve the pressure that is building up on Stephen's brain. The metal fragment also needs to be removed because if it slips even a millimeter, it could cut into the spine and leave him paralyzed."

I feel like I'm suffocating after hearing Maddox's words.

"How serious is this, Doc?" Nicco asks.

"I have to be honest with you. It's very serious."

I can tell that Maddox is being careful with his words, probably to keep from worrying us.

Even though I fear what the answer may be, I gather all my strength and ask, "What are Stephen's chances?"

"I can't answer that, Tony. I just know it is very serious. The best doctors are with him." He places his hand on my shoulder. "Believe me, they're doing everything they can for him. All any of us can do now is pray. I'll come out and give you updates as we get them."

Maddox leaves us.

"Have you eaten anything, sweetheart?" Sarah asks me.

"I can't eat right now."

"We'll see about that." She motions to Harvey to come close. "Would you and Nathan call Maria, our caterer, and see how soon she can get some food over here for all of us, especially for Tony and M?"

"You leave this to us, Sarah. Nathan and I are on it."

She smiles and then turns to Martha and me. "M, you may have gotten a quick pass out of this place, but you need to sit down and rest. And you, young man, are going to help me keep her in line, okay?"

"Okay." I know she's just trying to keep me busy taking care of Martha so I don't focus so much on what's happening to Stephen right now. I love her for it, but nothing is going to stop me from worrying about him. He's the love of my life, my future, my everything.

Please, Stephen. Come back to me.

MRS. CLARK and the rest of the vestry from Stephen's church rush into the waiting room. I'm thankful that my neighbors are here to fill them in on his condition.

"Father Stephen has to be okay," Mrs. Clark says, clearly shaken like the rest of us. "He just has to. He's such a wonderful young man."

"How long has it been since Maddox talked with us?" I quietly ask Sarah.

"Forty-two minutes, sweetheart."

Forty-two minutes. Very specific.

I nod, realizing that she's been focusing on the time even more than I have.

Every minute in this waiting area feels like an eternity.

AN HOUR LATER, I see Maddox walk into the waiting area in scrubs.

"What's happening?" I ask as everyone gathers around for the update on Stephen.

"Everything is looking very promising," he tells us. "Dr. Wilkinson was able to relieve the pressure on Stephen's brain with drugs and by lowering his body temperature. He will be monitoring Stephen's condition for any changes in pressure, but we don't look for that to happen."

"Oh, thank God," Mrs. Clark says.

Martha squeezes my hand.

I look at Maddox. "What's next for Stephen?"

"Dr. Wilkinson just began the surgery to remove the metal shard in Stephen's neck near his spine."

"How dangerous is this surgery?"

"I have to be honest with you, Tony. It's very dangerous. But we can't leave that shard where it is because where it's positioned, if it slips even a little, it can cause paralysis."

My gut tightens into a knot. "What if the shard slips when Dr. Wilkinson is trying to remove it? Could that leave Stephen paralyzed?"

"Yes. That's why it's so dangerous." Maddox looks me straight in the eyes. "But remember, Tony. Stephen has one of the best neuro-surgeons in the country. There isn't anyone I would trust more than Dr. Wilkinson with this kind of procedure. I'll be back to report to you when the surgery is over."

"Thank you, Doc," Nicco says.

We watch him leave, and I look once again at the time on my phone.

HARVEY AND NATHAN lead the caterer into the waiting area. There's enough food for our group and all the rest of the people with loved ones in the ER.

Sarah brings Martha and me each a plate. "Listen up, you two. You both have to eat. That's an order."

Martha gives her a mock salute. "Yes, ma'am."

"I'm not hungry," I tell them.

"I don't care if you're hungry or not, young man," Sarah says. "You need to be strong for Stephen. He's going to need you when this is over. Now, eat up."

"Okay." I take a few bites as an image of Stephen in a wheelchair without the ability to speak comes into view in my mind.

Stop thinking that way, Tony. I clench my jaw and close my eyes, willing the image away.

But whatever happens, I will be there for Stephen.

To all of our surprise, Father Grissom arrives.

"We weren't expecting you so soon." Trace and his husband, Luke, shake his hand. "Amarillo is at least a six-hour drive."

Father Grissom smiles. "I've made it in five, though I must confess I was speeding. But I didn't drive. One of my parishioners has his own plane and flew me here." He walks over to me and S & M. "Tell me, how is our boy doing?"

WHEN I SEE MADDOX AGAIN, I leap to my feet and rush to him. "How did it go?"

He smiles. "He's the toughest priest I've ever known. Surgery went perfectly. The brain swelling has lessened even more and the prognosis is good. It shouldn't be too long until they move him out of recovery and into a room in ICU."

S & M hug me, and everyone breathes a sigh of relief.

I look at Maddox. "So Stephen won't have any brain damage?"

"I wish I could give you an answer, but we won't know until he wakes up. My advice is for everyone to continue to pray. Stephen has done absolutely amazing so far."

Mrs. Clark turns to Father Grissom. "I think the doctor is right about us praying. Would you lead us in a prayer, Father?"

He nods. "Let's all join hands. Oh God, the strength of the weak and the comfort of those who suffer…"

As he prays, I squeeze S & M's hands. Though I don't believe, I'm touched as I see all these wonderful people coming together for Stephen.

I look at S & M, with their eyes closed and heads bowed. They've helped me when I didn't deserve it. I glance at Nicco, who is between Father Grissom and Mrs. Clark. Like S & M, his eyes are closed and his head is bowed. He never stopped believing even after everything he suffered. My big brother is tough as nails but has one of the most forgiving hearts I've ever known. I'm so glad that he and S & M are in my life. Without them, I wouldn't have survived.

I think about Stephen in that orphanage. He had no one. How did he turn out to be such a wonderful, amazing man?

Father Grissom ends the prayer.

I turn to Maddox. "When can I see Stephen?"

"As soon as he's settled, but brace yourself, because he has a long road to recovery."

I promise I'll be there for you, Stephen, no matter what. You will never be alone again.

Chapter 23

S *tephen*

I'M ALMOST to the end of the tunnel, almost to Father O'Malley and Ellen. I reach out my hand to them, but they won't take it.

"Is this paradise?" I ask them.

"It's not your time, sweetheart," she says.

Father O'Malley nods. "You have to go back."

"But I don't want to go back. There's so much beauty and peace here."

"Stephen, I love you," a voice from behind me whispers.

"That's Anthony," Father O'Malley tells me. "He needs you and you need him. Go back, son. We'll be waiting for both of you when it is your time."

Anthony

. . .

IT CRUSHES me seeing Stephen in such a state, hooked up to monitors, tubes, and an IV. His face is swollen and raw from the accident and both his eyes are black. He's covered in bandages and his arm is in a cast.

"Stephen, I love you," I whisper again in his ear. "I love you so much. I was so wrong. This is all my fault."

STEPHEN

FATHER O'MALLEY and Ellen vanish and the light begins to fade around me. I listen to Anthony's voice, which is echoing in the tunnel.

"This is all my fault. I love you so much. If I could go back and change things I would. I'm so sorry, sweetheart."

He loves me. I need to go back. I have to let him know that I don't blame him.

I turn around and rush down the tunnel, back to Anthony.

"I hope you can forgive me, my love." The heartache in his tone crushes me.

"It's not your fault," I repeat over and over with each step, praying he can hear me.

Anthony

I WATCH as the nurse checks Stephen's vitals.

"Father Stephen is still unconscious but it shouldn't be long before he wakes up," she tells me.

"How's he doing?" I ask her.

"He's doing great. Dr. Wilkinson should be here shortly to check on him."

"I see Stephen's lips are moving. Is he waking up?"

"He seems to be."

I lean down, placing my ear as close to his mouth as I can. I can't make out any words no matter how hard I try. "What is it, Stephen? What are you trying to say?"

"It's…not…your…fault." His words reach deep inside me like a healing salve.

"Can you hear me, Stephen? Are you awake?"

"Yes." His eyes open, and I feel like the sun just came up on the whole world. "Anthony. You're here. You're really here. I'm not dreaming."

"Yes, I'm here and I'm not going anywhere. I love you."

Stephen smiles. "And I love you."

He's not slurring his words. They are so clear. He must be okay. Happy tears of relief fall from my eyes. "Stephen, I have so much to say to you."

"Me, too. It's not your fault. None of it." His eyes close again. "My mouth is so dry."

"Would you like some ice, Father Stephen?" the nurse asks.

"Yes. Please."

"We don't want to tire him," the nurse says to me as she gives him some ice chips. "Let him wake up at his own pace. He probably won't remember any of this."

I nod, knowing I will remember for the both of us for the rest of my life.

I lean over and lightly kiss him on the lips. "Rest, my love. I'll be right here."

———

AS THE SUNLIGHT begins to filter through the window into the hospital room, I get up out of the chair that has been my bed for the past two nights to check on Stephen. He's resting peacefully. I'm so glad he's finally in his own room and out of ICU.

I sneak out to get a cup of coffee from the small kitchenette on this floor.

"Hey, Tony." Ken, one of Stephen's nurses, waves at me.

It's shift change.

"Hey, Ken."

"I hear Father Stephen is doing great," he says.

"He had a good night. Dr. Wilkinson says that he might even release him on Friday."

"That's great news. I'll be in shortly to get his vitals."

"Sounds good." I walk back into the room.

Stephen is still asleep.

I look around at all the flowers that fill the space. I even sent some home with S & M last night because there were so many. I'm sure I'll have to do the same again tonight.

I take a sip of coffee and begin reading the cards.

The red roses are from Mrs. Clark, who has been by every day. She's a wonderful woman.

The lilies are from Harvey and Nathan. Oliver and Adam sent the spring mix.

I come to the peace plant and read the card. It's from my mother.

DEAR STEPHEN,

You're in my prayers. Get well soon.

Love,

Carlotta

HER EXPRESSION of caring for Stephen moves me. She's also been here every day with Nicco. I never thought I would be able to forgive her, but somehow I have. Though our relationship will never be what it was when my dad was still alive, at least I'm open to building a friendship with her. The reason? Stephen steering Nicco and me to the Nar-Anon meetings. They've been eye opening, and I finally understand my mom and myself. The truth is, I never really stopped loving her.

"Where's my coffee, sweetheart?" Stephen asks.

I turn around and see him sitting up in the bed. I don't know how he does it with broken ribs and no help, but somehow he does. He's so strong.

I rush to the side of the bed. "I'll get you a cup and refill mine."

"Not before you give me a kiss."

I smile. "I didn't think you'd ever ask." I lean over and press my lips lightly against his.

"I can come back, guys," Ken says from the doorway. "But don't wear yourself out with your boyfriend, Father Stephen. We still have to take that morning lap around the floor."

"Come on in, Ken," I say. "I don't want to overtire our patient."

"What if your patient wants to be overtired?" Stephen says with a wicked grin.

"Too bad." It's great to see him doing so well.

"Fine. But we're not taking that walk until I have my coffee, fellas. Okay?"

Ken grins. "Yes, sir. I'll be back in ten minutes. Be ready."

"I will be. I bet I can do two full laps today."

He nods. "I bet you can, too."

"I better get your coffee," I say, walking out with Ken.

"He really is amazing, Tony. He's come so far so fast."

"Yes, he has." *We both have.*

I return with Stephen's coffee.

Since his right arm is in a cast, he takes it with his left hand.

After a sip, he says, "Mm. Perfect. This is what I call real medicine."

"I guess you'll have to take your walk before they bring your breakfast."

"Hospital breakfast." He frowns. "You know what I'd really like? A sausage, egg, and cheese biscuit."

"Nicco is coming up." I bring out my phone. "I'll text him to bring us both one on his way over."

"Thank you, sweetheart. Be sure to tell him I need lots of grape jelly."

"Already did," I say, tucking my cell back into my pocket.

"You're the best." He places his cup on his tray and takes my hand. "Anthony, you really do need to get some rest. Why don't you spend the night at your apartment? I'll be fine on my own."

"This overstuffed chair makes a good bed. And S & M have brought me a change of clothes every day. And so far, none of the nurses have turned me in for using your shower. This is a dream vacation, if you ask me."

"Oh, really?" He grins. "And I thought you were taking me to Hawaii."

"Some day I will, but you have to get better first."

"I am getting better, sweetheart. Don't you think I look better than most people who have been hit by a bus?"

I laugh. "Why do you keep asking everyone that?"

"Because I do look good, don't I?"

"Yes, you do. You look amazing. Although you're the first person I've ever seen who was hit by a bus."

"Well, if I do look good, Anthony, it's because you're my best medicine." He takes a sip. "And this coffee comes in a good second."

"Yeah. I beat out the coffee for the championship. I couldn't be happier."

He smiles.

Ken walks back in. "Okay, Father Stephen. You ready to go?"

"I am if you are. I hope you can keep up." Stephen lets out a little groan as we help him out of the bed. "I'm okay, guys. It's just that these broken ribs smart sometimes."

I'm so impressed at his strength and tenacity. He's determined to get back to normal as soon as he can.

After the second lap, he looks at Ken and me. "One more."

"If you're strong enough."

"I'm strong enough, and you know as well as I do that walking prevents pneumonia in patients."

"Let's do it," I say, and we take another lap.

When we get back to the room, Stephen is smiling, but I can tell he's worn out.

"I told you I could do it."

"Yes, you did," Ken says. "Good for you. Now let's get you back to bed."

"Be sure to write that down so Dr. Wilkinson will not change his mind about me going home Friday."

"I sure will and I'll circle it to make sure he sees it." Ken fluffs Stephen's pillow. "I'll be back later, guys."

"Thanks for everything," Stephen says.

Ken gives us the thumbs-up signal. "Good job, Father. You'll be running a marathon before you know it."

He walks out of the room.

"Anthony, come over here and kiss me."

"Sure, but what if I want more than one?"

"That'll work. I do have an upper lip and a lower lip. Two for the price of one."

"You are so romantic, Stephen Norelli. That's an offer I can't refuse." I lean in and kiss him. "I love you so much, Stephen."

"Do you love me enough to marry me?" he asks me, pulling me down for another kiss.

"As soon as you are well, we'll make plans to get married. I promise. I want to spend the rest of my life with you."

"Well, why not get married now? We're already living together in this hospital room."

"You can't be serious."

"I'm very serious. I've waited so long for you, Anthony. I don't want to wait another minute." He touches my cheek. "Father Grissom is coming today at noon."

"But we need a license, Stephen, and I believe there's a three-day waiting period in Texas."

"I know. But Harvey is bringing a judge friend of his, too. A judge can waive the waiting period."

"How long have you been planning this?"

"Since they moved me out of ICU." He grins. "I've had a little help working out the details. And that hasn't been easy because you are in the room almost all the time. Have you noticed that I always send you for coffee when we have visitors?"

"You devil."

"Guilty. But I got most of it worked out yesterday when you were taking your shower. So, if you say yes to me, and I am certain you will, the service starts at noon. Nicco is your best man and S & M are my best women. We already have the flowers. What do you say? Will you marry me?"

"Like you've given me a choice, Father Stephen, but of course I will marry you." I kiss him. "You've made me the happiest man in the world."

"No, you've made me the happiest man in the world. I love you, Anthony Mantonvani."

I hear cheering coming from the door. When I turn, I see Ken, Dr. Wilkinson, and Nicco applauding.

"Do you have our breakfast order yet, Nicco?" Stephen says.

"I sure do." He steps forward and holds up a sack. "And six grape jelly packets too for my wonderful brother-in-law to be."

S & M walk into Stephen's room with their arms full. They are wearing beautiful pale blue dresses. Nicco and I give each of them a hug.

"You two look gorgeous today," I say.

"Thank you, sweetheart," Sarah says. "It is your wedding after all."

She and Martha put down their packages.

"We have some things for you boys and your wedding." Martha kisses Stephen on the cheek. "You look marvelous."

"I feel marvelous. I'm marrying the man of my dreams today."

"That makes two of us," I say.

"You know the old saying for weddings?" Martha asks. "Something old, something new, something borrowed, something blue?"

"Oh, yes," Stephen says. "I've officiated at enough weddings to have heard it before."

"I've never officiated at any wedding, but I think everyone knows that saying." I can feel the excitement building inside me. Only a couple of hours before Stephen and I say our I dos. "Why do you ask? Isn't that about what the bride is supposed to wear on her wedding day? Neither of us are brides."

"So?" Martha winks. "Let's make the tradition fit for you two. It's about love anyway, right?"

"Right," Stephen and I say together.

"Now M?"

She nods. "You bet."

Sarah hands me a package, and Martha gives its twin to Stephen.

"This covers the new and blue part," Sarah says.

We open the boxes and find ties that are the same pale blue as their dresses.

Stephen grabs Martha's hand. "Thank you."

"Yes, thank you both," I say.

"And here's one for you, Nicco," Sarah says. "You are Stephen's best man."

"Thank you, ladies. You're the best."

Martha grins. "Yes, we are. Now, about the borrowed part." She reaches in her purse and pulls out two champagne flutes. "These are from our wedding, boys. You won't be wearing them like the original tradition, but who cares? Not me. You will be using them at the reception."

"Reception?" Stephen's eyes widen. "What reception?"

"You'll see, sweetheart." Martha's eyes are brimming with tears. "Now for the best gift of all. For something old." She hands each of us tiny boxes.

We open them and see a ring inside each box.

"These rings belonged to Malcolm, and S and I know that he would want you to use these for your wedding rings. We knew you wouldn't have time to buy any, and this is a way to have Malcolm with you on this special day."

"With all of us," I say, remembering the man who saved me from self-destruction and ruining my life. I miss him so much. I kiss them both and then hold Stephen's hand. "Thank you. This means so much to me."

"You have made us both so very happy," he says. "You've done so much."

"We're not through yet." Martha looks around the room. "S, we have our jobs cut out for us on this one."

Sarah salutes her. "Reporting for duty, General."

We all laugh.

"Stephen, lie back and rest," Martha orders. "You've got a big day ahead of you. Anthony, your only job is to make sure he does."

"Yes, ma'am."

"Nicco, you're with S and me. We need to make room and get some of these flowers out of here."

"I'm your man. Which flowers do you want me to take?"

"Let's start with all the roses first."

I look at Stephen. "See what you started."

He smiles and squeezes my hand. "I love you."

"I love you, too."

Chapter 24

"What time is it?" Stephen asks me, adjusting his tie.

I look at the time on my phone. "11:55 a.m."

"Where is everyone?" He moved to the chair an hour ago, anxious for the ceremony.

"I don't know. I'll check out in the hall. Maybe I'll see someone." I open the door. "No one out here."

"Why don't you call Nicco? Maybe he knows something."

"Good idea, sweetheart." I bring out my phone, but before I have a chance to call my brother, I see him, Father Grissom, and Ken heading my way with a wheelchair. "Something is definitely going on."

Father Grissom shakes my hand. "Are you both ready to head to the church? It's almost time."

"Church?" I shake my head. "I'm confused."

Nicco places his hand on my shoulder. "Wedding day jitters, probably. Just leave everything to us."

"Father Stephen, would you like me to help you into the car?" Ken asks, motioning to the wheelchair.

"What model car is this?" Stephen grins. "It's a beauty."

"It's a brand new Lexus, right off the lot."

"I think I can manage on my own, but thank you." He sits down in the wheelchair and we're off. "Do you know anything about this, Anthony?"

"No. I have no idea what's going on."

They lead us to the hospital chapel on the third floor. We hear music coming from inside.

"Anthony, does that sound like Red Shimmer?"

"I think it is." I smile. "You know that S & M had a lot to do with this surprise, and they are big fans of Chad, Josh, and Franki."

Nicco and Father Grissom open the double doors to the chapel and I wheel Stephen inside. The room is filled to capacity with our friends and family for our wedding.

S & M are standing in the front and motion us forward, while Red Shimmer starts playing the wedding march. Everyone stands as we go down the aisle.

Nicco and Father Grissom follow us down to the front and each take their places.

"You may be seated," Father Grissom says to those who came to celebrate with us. "We are gathered here to witness the joining of two incredible young men."

I'm really doing this. I'm really marrying the man of my dreams.

As Father Grissom continues the service, I look in Stephen's eyes and realize that today is the beginning, *our beginning.*

"Who presents Stephen and Anthony?" Father Grissom asks.

"We do," S & M and Nicco say together in unison.

"Do you promise to love, respect, and pray for Stephen and Anthony, and to do all in your power to stand with them in the life they will share?"

"We do."

He turns to Stephen. "Do you freely and unreservedly offer yourself to Anthony?"

"I do."

"Will you live together in holiness and faithfulness so long as you both shall live?"

"I will."

"Do you take this man to be your lawfully wedded husband?"

"I do."

I'm overwhelmed with joy, hearing Stephen say these vows.

Father Grissom turns to me. And I repeat the same to him.

After we exchange rings, he says in that big booming voice of his, "I now pronounce that these two wonderful men, Stephen Norelli and Anthony Mantonvani, are bound to one another as husbands for life in a holy covenant, as long as they both shall live. Amen"

"Amen," everyone says together.

"You may kiss your husband," Father Grissom says.

I wrap my arms around Stephen.

"Ouch."

"Sorry, sweetheart. I forgot about your ribs."

He grins and we kiss.

Everyone cheers.

"We're really married, Stephen. I'm married to you and you're married to me."

He laughs. "That's kind of how it works, sweetheart."

"I love you."

"I love you, too."

I WHEEL Stephen into the room where S & M are hosting our wedding reception. We learned from Nicco that Jaris and Maddox got the hospital to turn over this executive conference room for our party.

"How did S & M do all this?" Stephen asks me.

"I lived with them a long time and they never told me where their superpowers come from. I decided they were angels in disguise."

"Oh, really? It sounds like you're starting to believe in a higher power, Anthony."

"I'll say this, sweetheart. There are certainly a lot of wonderful people who do believe, like yourself, who I love and respect. I believe in them. And I definitely believe in us."

"That's all that matters to me, my love."

"Everyone, the happy couple has arrived," Mrs. Clark announces.

Another cheer.

"Look at the spread of food," Stephen says. "I'm famished. That breakfast sandwich is long gone."

"Mine, too. You want me to get you a plate?" I ask, concerned he may be getting tired.

"I can manage." He gets out of the wheelchair and motions Dr. Wilkinson's direction. "Besides, he needs to see how strong I am. I'm busting out of this place on Friday come hell or high water."

"Yes, you are." I walk with him to the table with all the food.

I see O'Brien and his fiancée standing next to Oliver and Adam. We're all so proud of Oliver getting that assignment with the FBI. He'll be heading up a team in Dallas.

Behind them are LaShaya and her husband Hayden, with their little girl. It's hard to believe that they'll be moving to Sweden later this year. God, we're going to miss them so much. Her brother Brexton will remain in Unit B. He's still in college. It's awful about how his parents treat him since he told them he was gay.

Eli and Jackson come up to Stephen and me.

"Have you heard?" Jackson asks. "Eli just got promoted to captain at the fire department."

"That's great news, guys," Stephen says. "Congratulations."

"And congratulations to you both." Eli puts his arm around Jackson. "I can attest to how wonderful married life can be."

"Guys, did you see that?" Stephen asks.

"See what, sweetheart?"

"Look."

I glance Harrison and Ava's direction. "He's patting her belly."

"I know. Is she pregnant?"

"I bet she is, but don't say anything. It might be a secret."

Ava is grinning from ear to ear. *Yes, she's pregnant.* She and

Harrison are sitting next to Trace and Luke with their little boy, Micky. They all live together in the combined units of D and E.

"Anthony, look at our Mockingbird Place family. We're so lucky."

I kiss him. "I'm so lucky."

Chapter 25

S *everal months later*

STEPHEN and I walk into our hotel suite in Maui. The room is amazing and has a spectacular view of the ocean. He's completely recovered from the accident. Dr. Wilkinson, Jaris, and Maddox were amazed at how quick his progress was. I wasn't. I know how determined my man can be.

"Wow," Stephen says, pulling me into his arms. "You did good."

"What can I say? Maybe I'll give up fighting and become a honeymoon specialist."

He laughs. That sound always fills me with such joy. We spot a bottle of champagne and an ordinary white box on the table.

"You?" he asks.

I shake my head, picking up the card next to the goodies.

He pops the cork and fills the two champagne flutes. "Go ahead and read it, sweetheart."

. . .

DEAR SWEET BOYS,

We wish you the best time on your honeymoon. But how are we going to survive without you for two weeks? We already miss you!

Lose yourself in the bliss of romance.

Each day you'll receive a special gift and note from your friends and loved ones here at Mockingbird Place. Of course, we demanded the first day and no one dared to deny us.

Hope you enjoy the bottle of champagne and donuts.

This is the beginning of the rest of your life together.

Love,

Mama S & Mama M

I OPEN the box of donuts. "Chocolate icing with sprinkles."

"Those two wonderful women think of everything. This is better than I could have dreamed of."

"You're better than I could have ever dreamed of, sweetheart." I pull him into my arms and devour his mouth. "Give me one of those donuts. I want to see what you look and taste like in sprinkles."

"Oh, you do, do you?" Stephen steps back. "You'll have to catch me first."

"Oh, I'll catch you." I grab a donut out of the box and chase him around the room until I get him cornered. "Whatcha going to do now, big boy?"

"Well, you got one thing right." He grabs my hand and puts it on his crotch. I can feel his hard cock through his jeans. "Is that big enough for you?"

"I'm not sure." I get down on my knees. "I need a closer look to be sure."

"Hey, it's your honeymoon too." He unzips his jeans. "Who am I to deny you anything?"

I pull down his jeans, leaving him in his black boxers. His dick is so hard and long that it sticks out of the elastic waist.

He removes the rest of his clothes, including the boxers. I gaze at the most incredible body I've ever seen. He's ripped from head to toe.

Stephen grabs his dick and waves it at me. "Well, Anthony?"

"You already know what I think about your cock, sweetheart."

He smiles. "Yeah, but I want to hear it again."

"Fine. Your cock is the most beautiful thing I've ever seen. Satisfied?"

"Hardly," Stephen says. "I want to know if you like it better than those donuts."

"Hey, I *like* donuts, but I *love* the taste of your cock." I toss the donut aside, forgetting all about it, and swallow the treat I really desire.

As I swirl my tongue over the head of his dick, I cup his balls and give them a little squeeze.

"That's it, Anthony. So good. Mm."

I dive down his shaft until the head of his cock hits the back of my throat. My reward is a slew of wicked groans from his beautiful lips.

I bob up and down him as he claws my shoulders.

"I'm getting…so…so…close."

I suck on him hard, hollowing out my cheeks and tightening my lips around his dick.

"Ohh!" he yells, and then I feel him shoot into my thirsty mouth.

I drink down every drop.

"I win," Stephen says.

"What do you mean you win?" I stand and face him. "I won. I got to have you first."

"No. That's not right. I got to enjoy your mouth first, Anthony Mantonvani. So I win."

"So you're making all the rules today?"

"I sure am, today. All the rules. Every last one. Tomorrow? Maybe I'll let you make the rules and be the referee." He pushes me into a chair. "Right now, let me show you how a winner does it." He rips off all my clothes, licking every inch of my skin.

"Oh, my God, I married a winner. Wow! A gold medal, blue ribbon winner."

He laughs. "Yeah, but you haven't seen anything yet."

As he rakes his tongue over the head of my hard cock, a blazing heat rises up inside me. "Cross that finish line, winner. Take me all the way."

"Oh, I will. Trust me."

Feeling his lips tighten around me drives me wild with desire. "Damn, you're good at that. So freaking good."

Stephen continues sucking on me until I can't hold back any longer. "Fuuuck!"

My entire body tenses, every muscle tightening, every nerve ending firing. I come, sending my seed down his throat.

He stands, lifting his arms above his head. "I'm the champ. Say it."

"Winner? Okay. Champ?" I grin. "I'm the champ."

I leap from the chair, grab him, and shove him onto the bed. I press my lips to his, sending my hungry tongue into his greedy mouth.

"You're mine, Stephen. All mine." I flip him on his stomach and lick his ass, getting it ready for my entrance.

"No fair. You're cheating. Mm. Don't stop."

"Who's the champ?" I ask, fingering him.

"I'm not sure." He laughs wickedly.

"Oh, really?" I thrust my finger into him, sliding it in and out. "How about now?"

"I might become a believer."

"I'll show you who is the champ." I grab my cock and guide it into his body.

He groans. "Oh, yeah. You're the champ. That's…oh…yes…"

I plunge deeper into him. Watching him fist the sheets thrills me. I want to pleasure him to the very brink of sanity, so I thrust in and out of him. Again and again.

When I feel myself getting close, I whisper in his ear, "Come for the champ, baby. Come for me."

"Ahh!"

I can feel his body spasm on my cock, and that pushes me over the top. "Oh, yeah! Yes. Yes."

I kiss the back of his neck. "I love you, husband."

"I love you, too."

Chapter 26

S *tephen*

AS I WALK UP to the lectern to deliver my sermon, I see Anthony come in with a couple I don't recognize. He leads them to the pew where S & M are sitting with his mother and Nicco.

During the entire service, my curiosity grows. My husband loves to surprise me. Are these people part of a surprise? I see the woman cling to the man. There are tears in her eyes.

Did my sermon touch her that much? It was about God's unshakable love for us.

Today is my one-year anniversary at the Episcopal Church of the Beloved Disciple. Mrs. Clark has organized quite the party to celebrate after the service. I can't believe how wonderful my life is. I have an amazing man who loves me, a parish I adore, and I live in the most incredible place in the world with people who have become my family.

After the recessional, I stand in my regular spot in the narthex to shake hands with everyone.

Anthony is at the end of the line with that couple. Who are they? I've never seen them before. They're an attractive couple and look to be around forty years old.

Finally, I shake hands with the last parishioner and turn to Anthony. "Hey, honey. Who are your friends?"

He smiles and grabs my hand. "Sweetheart, this is Dave and Erin Blue. They're your parents."

"My what? Parents?" I shake off the shock. "I don't mean to be rude, but how do you know that?"

"You remember Sam Newsome?"

"Yeah. The PI that works for Jaris's parents. He helped clear Nicco's name."

"He sure did, and he helped me find your birth parents."

Tears fall from the woman's eyes. "Stephen, we've been looking for you for years."

Tears also fall from the man's eyes. "Thank God, we found you."

"I'm still in shock. I can't believe this." I turn to Anthony. "You did this for me."

"Yes, I did."

"Our parents forced us to give you up," Erin says. "We were so young."

"Stephen, we really didn't have a choice." Dave looks me in the eyes. "But we never stopped loving you or each other."

"You got married."

"We did," they say in unison.

Dave smiles. "Our parents did their best to keep us apart, but our love was stronger. So as soon I turned nineteen and Erin turned eighteen, we eloped."

"I know this must be very hard to take in," she says. "But know that we want you and Anthony to be a part of our family, if you'll have us. Your brother and sister really want to meet you."

"A brother and a sister? How old are they? What are their names?"

"Your brother is Mike and just turned sixteen," Dave says. "Andrea is thirteen, and has your eyes."

"This is amazing. Wow." My heart feels like it's soaring into the stratosphere. "I heard about you when I was in the system. They told me some of your story at the orphanage. You were so young. I have never blamed you. I'm so glad you came."

As they wrap their arms around me, I look at Anthony, amazed that he made this happen for me. I have a father and a mother. A sister and a brother. And a man who loves me with all his heart. A real family.

I will never be alone again.

About the Author

Lee Swift, who writes under several pen names including Kris Cook, creates novels, short stories, screenplays and more.

With an unquenchable thirst to experience all his life journey has to offer, Lee and hubby love travel but still call Dallas, Texas home.

Join [HERE] to get updates on Lee.

Also by Lee Swift

Novels

Morvicti Blood *(Supernatural Thriller)*

Cupid's Arrow *(Gay Fantasy Romance)*

Three to Play *(Menage MMF Romance)*

(All series listed in best reading order)

Mockingbird Place

(Gay Romance Series)

The Marine in Unit A

The Cowboy in Unit E

The Fireman in Unit C

The Doctor in Unit H

The Fighter in Unit J

Holiday Beaus (Novella)

The Musician in Unit G

The Cop in Unit B

Wolf Pack

(Menage MFM Romance Trilogy)

Secret Cravings

Primal Desires

Delicious Hunger

Eternal Trio Series

(Gay Menage Fantasy Romance)

Levi's Rogues

Perfection

www.ingramcontent.com/pod-product-compliance
Lightning Source LLC
Chambersburg PA
CBHW021008180626
46814CB00003B/1191